WHAT'S GOING ON IN LISA'S FAMILY?

Lisa woke up at dawn. Her room was gray in the early morning light, and the house was as quiet as it had been the night before. She looked at her watch. It was 6:15. She didn't have to be at school until eight. If she hurried, she could stop by CARL on her way to school and check on PJ. Her parents wouldn't be up for another half hour. It would mean she'd miss them, but PJ was important, and she was sure they'd understand.

Lisa hurried through her morning routine, then picked up her book bag and went downstairs. She scribbled a note for her mother and headed for the front door. As she passed the den, she noticed a pile of blankets on the sofa, and then realized it wasn't really a pile of blankets. It was her father with some blankets on him. He must have gotten in really late the night before and hadn't wanted to wake up Lisa's mother. She blew him a silent kiss and went out the front door.

Other books you will enjoy

CAMY BAKER'S HOW TO BE POPULAR
IN THE SIXTH GRADE by Camy Baker

HORSE CRAZY (The Saddle Club #1) by Bonnie Bryant

AMY, NUMBER SEVEN (Replica #1) by Marilyn Kaye

PURSUING AMY (Replica #2) by Marilyn Kaye

ANASTASIA ON HER OWN by Lois Lowry

THE BOYS START THE WAR/
THE GIRLS GET EVEN by Phyllis Reynolds Naylor

the SADDLE CLUB

STRAY HORSE

BONNIE BRYANT

A SKYLARK BOOK
NEW YORK • TORONTO • LONDON • SYDNEY • AUCKLAND

RL: 3.6, AGES 008–012

STRAY HORSE
A Bantam Skylark Book / September 2001

ISBN: 0-553-48742-6

Published simultaneously in the United States and Canada

Bantam Skylark is an imprint of Random House Children's Books.
SKYLARK BOOK, BANTAM BOOKS, and the rooster colophon are
registered trademarks of Random House, Inc. Bantam Books, 1540
Broadway, New York, New York 10036.

PRINTED IN THE UNITED STATES OF AMERICA

OPM   10 9 8 7 6 5 4 3 2 1

Lisa Atwood opened her eyes. In the gray light that filtered through the window, it took her a moment to orient herself. She was home. It was a Saturday morning. Nothing unusual in that. She glanced at the clock on her bedside table. It was 6:30. She calculated backward. She wanted to get to the stable by eight. Half an hour to shower and dress, fifteen minutes to eat, fifteen minutes to walk over there. She could sleep for another few minutes.

"Good morning, sleepy."

Lisa had almost forgotten that one of her best friends, Carole Hanson, had slept over.

"Good morning to you," Lisa said. "Been up long?"

"No, I just woke up," said Carole. "Is it time to get up?"

1

"Not quite," Lisa said.

"We promised Stevie we'd call her at seven," Carole reminded Lisa.

"We've got half an hour, then," Lisa said, pulling the covers up securely under her chin and enjoying the tranquility of the morning. She loved it when everything was quiet in her house. A car door slammed. Lisa turned on her side.

"We should call her at quarter of and then again at seven," Carole said.

Lisa laughed. "Maybe we should have started calling her at five o'clock!"

Stevie—short for Stephanie—Lake was the third of their inseparable threesome. Although the three of them were very different from one another in many ways, they had a common bond that was far stronger than their differences: They were all utterly, totally, absolutely nuts about horses. They'd discovered this bond soon after they'd met and had decided to formalize it by declaring themselves the first members of their own club: The Saddle Club. They gave themselves only two rules. The first was one none of them had ever been tempted to break: They had to be horse-crazy. The second had been a little dicier. They'd declared that they always had to be willing to help one another out, no matter what.

Sometimes it seemed that Stevie was the one who needed the most help. Her friends liked to describe her as lots of fun and a magnet for trouble. Stevie had three brothers, one older, one younger, and her twin, Alex. A lot of the time when she was getting into trouble it was because she was determined to right some wrong she felt they'd done her. The Lake household was a minefield of practical jokes the boys and Stevie played on one another. More than once, Stevie had had to explain to her teacher that she really *had* finished her math homework, but she'd done it with a disappearing-ink pen, and if the teacher would just put the paper in lemon juice . . .

Stevie was wild, fun, funny, and irrepressible. She was also a sound sleeper. Calling her to be sure she woke up in time for their Pony Club meeting was one of the easiest things her friends ever had to do for her.

While Stevie was prone to practical jokes and wild schemes—and her will was almost always good—her results were uneven at best. She often complained that her grades in school would be better if she didn't have to spend so much of her class time in the principal's office. Her teachers didn't see it that way.

Lisa was the absolute opposite in that regard. She never handed in her assignments late, she never forgot to study for a test, and she never got less than an A on anything.

3

Her clothes were always clean and neatly ironed, and her hair always stayed in place. She was calm, rational, and logical. Sometimes she took on more than she could handle, but her friends were always there to help her out when that happened. Lisa was the newest rider of the three, but as their instructor, Max Regnery, said, she was a very fast learner. Within a short time she'd just about caught up with the years of experience that Carole and Stevie had.

Carole was the best rider of the three of them, and if they were all horse-crazy, Carole was the horse-craziest. She'd been riding since she was very young. Her father, a colonel in the Marines, had had to move from base to base when she was a little girl. The bases may have been different from one another, but they all had stables either on them or nearby, and Carole learned at an early age that when everything was changing around her, horses were her anchor. That had comforted and helped her through those moves and through her mother's illness and death a few years earlier. She and her father lived not far from Quantico, Virginia, where he was now stationed. Quantico was near the town of Willow Creek, where Carole and her friends rode at Pine Hollow Stables and where the girls went to school. But Carole's house wasn't within walking distance of the stable, so she liked to sleep over at one of her friends' houses when she wanted to be at Pine

Hollow early on a Saturday morning. Both Stevie and Lisa were always happy to have her. In fact, the three of them were planning a sleepover at Stevie's house for that night so that they could get to the stable early on Sunday morning as well. Sleepovers usually meant extended Saddle Club meetings, at which the girls could do their next-to-favorite thing, which was talking about horses. Their favorite, of course, was actually riding them.

Carole pushed the covers away and reached for the phone. After three rings, a sleepy-sounding Stevie picked up.

"Fifteen-minute warning," Carole said. She hung up before Stevie could say something she might regret. "I'll shower first," Carole said to Lisa.

Lisa smiled. Like Carole, she was eager to get to Pine Hollow. But unlike Carole, she was glad for another few minutes in bed.

While Carole showered, Lisa listened for sounds in the house. Her parents were usually up early on Saturdays, but she didn't hear any movement downstairs. She had a few minutes of utter calm and peace. Who knew what the rest of the day would bring?

When Carole emerged from the bathroom, Lisa went in, leaving Carole to make the final, dire call to Stevie. Twenty minutes later the two girls went downstairs together.

The lights were on, but the house was unusually quiet. Lisa's father was sitting in the den, reading the newspaper, a glass of orange juice on the table near him.

"Good morning, Daddy," Lisa said.

"Morning, Mr. Atwood," said Carole.

"Good morning, girls," he said, then shuffled his paper.

Lisa and Carole went into the kitchen. Mrs. Atwood wasn't there, but there were signs she had been. The kitchen table was set for them for breakfast; the coffee was made.

Lisa selected a variety of cereals from the cabinet, poured juice for herself and Carole, and invited her father to join them.

"I'll just read the paper," he said, remaining in the den.

"Where's Mom?"

"Hmph," he answered.

Lisa shrugged and sat down. They were out of milk. She put the cereal back and took some bread out of the refrigerator to make toast. She popped four slices into the toaster, and when they emerged she and Carole buttered them and spread on some jam. Breakfast was finished in just a few minutes. The girls then took some time to scrounge up sandwich fixings for lunch.

It didn't take long to assemble a couple of tuna fish sandwiches, slice some carrots, and find some cookies and chips and a can of soda for each of them. Carole was putting a napkin in each bag when the kitchen door swung open and Mrs. Atwood marched in, her face stony, apparently unaware of the presence of either Carole or Lisa.

"There!" she sputtered toward the door to the den. "Now you've got the milk for your coffee. Are you satisfied?"

She put the milk in the refrigerator and slammed the door. Then she poured herself a cup of coffee and sat at the kitchen table, scowling.

Mr. Atwood came in, poured himself some coffee, and went to the refrigerator for the milk.

Carole was uncomfortable with witnessing such a scene and found herself wishing she'd stayed in the shower a lot longer. Maybe she could run upstairs and get back in. Or maybe a hole in the floor would open up and swallow her. Another look around and she realized it wouldn't have made any difference. Nobody seemed to have the slightest idea that she was there.

"I got my history project back yesterday," Lisa said brightly. "Remember the one about Julius Caesar? With the model of the Roman senate?" Nobody said anything, but Lisa continued. "I got an A on it." Still no response. "I had to work really hard on that one—boy, you can't imagine how hard it was to build a model of the Roman senate. It made a big difference that we'd been in Rome on vacation. So thank you guys for that!"

7

"That's nice," her father said.

"Oh, and I got a perfect score on the spelling test."

Lisa's parents didn't seem to register the fact that their daughter was speaking to them. They were each glaring at different sections of the newspaper.

Carole wanted to help. "You always get perfect scores on spelling tests. Every other test, too!" she teased.

"Yes," said Mrs. Atwood.

Carole squirmed.

"Well, I've got a science test coming up next week," Lisa said. "It's in earth science and that's a really difficult subject for me. I've got to study especially hard for it."

No response.

"What do you think we'll be working on at Horse Wise today?" Carole asked. Horse Wise was the name of their Pony Club.

"Max said it would be something different. That man really loves surprises!" Lisa said. "I can hardly wait."

The stilted conversation and the stony set of parents was more than Carole could bear. She stood up, getting ready to leave.

"Isn't it time for you to leave for the—uh—stable?" Mrs. Atwood asked.

Carole's thought exactly. "Come on, Lisa. Let's get our stuff," she said.

The girls put their dishes in the sink. Normally Carole would have rinsed them and put them in the dishwasher, but she suspected Lisa's parents wouldn't have noticed if she'd flown them across the room Frisbee-style, and Carole simply couldn't wait to get out of the kitchen.

She followed her friend upstairs, unsure of what to say. She'd seen parents have arguments before. She'd seen parents and kids have arguments. But she couldn't remember seeing anything that cold-blooded—and all about a carton of *milk*? Well, that was the point, she suspected; it wasn't about a carton of milk. Arguments could be like icebergs. Only one-seventh was above water.

"Lisa . . . ," Carole began.

"Do you remember where I put my boots?" Lisa asked.

"In your closet on the floor, where you always put them," said Carole.

A few minutes later Carole followed Lisa back downstairs, carrying everything they would need for their Pony Club meeting and the lesson that would follow. Lisa's parents were still in the kitchen, still glaring at their newspapers.

Lisa gave them each a hug and a kiss. Carole thanked them for letting her stay over.

"Have a good day," Mrs. Atwood said, but her smile looked forced.

Carole thought that as soon as she got out of the house,

she just might have a good day, and in any case she was certain she was going to have a better day than Lisa's parents.

She couldn't do anything about that, she knew, but she could do something abut Lisa. It took her a while to assemble her thoughts. She wanted Lisa to know that it was okay, Lisa shouldn't be embarrassed about her parents' behavior and Carole didn't care anyway. She remembered that her own parents used to have arguments sometimes. What she couldn't remember, and wouldn't say to Lisa, was ever seeing her parents seething like that.

"Listen, Lisa," Carole said carefully. "It's okay and you don't have anything to be embarrassed about."

"What?" Lisa asked.

"You know—that," Carole said. "The milk thing."

"My dad likes milk in his coffee," Lisa said.

It wasn't the words as much as the tone that said Lisa didn't want to talk—didn't think there was anything to talk about. That made Carole think about icebergs again. *Just one-seventh*, she told herself.

"I can't wait to see what Max is up to," said Lisa. "I mean, what could it be?"

Carole let the first topic drop. If Lisa wanted to forget about it, if she wasn't upset, that was good enough for Carole. "I can't wait, either," she said, and she meant it, too.

2

"WELL, LOOK WHO made it!" Lisa joked, spotting Stevie, who was waiting for them in the driveway at Pine Hollow.

"Thanks for waking me up. I wouldn't have missed this for anything!"

"What?" Lisa asked.

"This meeting," said Stevie. "It's going to be soooo much fun."

"They all are," Carole told her, heading toward the stable. "Because they're all about horses."

"Well, this meeting isn't, but it's still going to be fun," said Stevie.

"So what's the story?" Lisa asked, linking arms with

Stevie and following Carole toward the cluster of kids already waiting for the meeting to begin.

"I'll give you a hint," Stevie said. "It starts with a C and ends with *A-R-L*."

"Judy's here?" Carole asked eagerly, scanning the grounds for Judy Barker, Pine Hollow's equine veterinarian. *CARL* stood for *County Animal Rescue League*. It was a local shelter run by volunteers for abandoned and ill animals. Whenever the animal in question was a horse, Judy volunteered her time, and Pine Hollow's students often helped out, learning about animal care and veterinary medicine as they pitched in.

"Nope," Stevie said. "It's Doc Tock."

Doc Tock was actually Dr. Takamura, but her patients' owners usually shortened both the names. She was a small-animal vet. In her regular practice that usually meant dogs and cats, occasional parakeets and hamsters. At CARL, it could mean anything from aardvarks to wildcats.

Max called the meeting to order and indicated that all the students should come over to where he and Doc Tock were standing. He began by introducing Doc Tock, though most of the students already knew her.

"We're going to do something a little different today, kids, and I'm going to let Doc Tock tell you all about it."

The students fell silent, eager to hear what was going on.

"You were probably all in town for the big rainstorm last week," she began. Lisa thought back to the violent storm, with strong winds, thunder, and lightning. Doc Tock continued. "There was a lot of obvious damage to the land. What isn't quite so obvious to many people is that a storm like that is as destructive to the wildlife as it is to the woodlands. CARL has been inundated with new residents. We've got birds, squirrels, raccoons, a skunk, two snakes, a deer with a broken leg, plus several feral cats and the usual assortment of pet dogs, cats, and hamsters. In short, we're overwhelmed, and we need some help. Max suggested that you all might be willing to come to our aid."

"We're not doctors," said May.

"I don't expect you to be," said Doc Tock. "I'm just hoping you'll be able to help with feeding and cleaning and maybe assist Judy and me in a few things. It's just for this morning. Can I count on you?"

"You bet," Carole said enthusiastically. Although there was nothing she loved more than horses, other animals were close seconds and she was more than willing to help—even if it meant missing out on a couple of hours with her favorites.

It turned out that just about everybody was willing to

13

pitch in at CARL. The one exception, which surprised nobody, was Veronica diAngelo. Veronica was Pine Hollow's richest and snobbiest rider. Her idea of helping someone out at Pine Hollow was to let the stable hands know there was a job to do. That way she never broke a sweat—or a fingernail.

Veronica was left to ride her horse in the schooling ring while all the other students followed Doc Tock down the street to CARL. As far as The Saddle Club was concerned, there were a lot of great things about CARL. One was that it was within walking distance of Pine Hollow.

All it took was one look around for the girls to realize how much they were needed. The place was a mess.

"Okay," Lisa said, putting her naturally logical self in the lead. "We've got to clean out all these cages and then begin cleaning and feeding the animals themselves. Let's form teams of three. One, two, three; one, two, three." She had seven teams formed before Doc Tock and Max had followed the last stragglers through the door. "The first team will start with the birdcages; teams two and three, you get the small woodland animals, be careful of the skunk. Four and five, you clean out the cats. Six and seven, we get the dogs. Okay, we'll start at the far end."

Stevie enjoyed watching Lisa in action. She wasn't a loud or pushy person; she wasn't even a particularly strong

14

leader. It was just that she was so utterly logical that everybody followed her lead. Stevie could have done the same thing, she told herself, but it would have taken her a half hour to figure out what size the teams should be and how to sort them around the large building. Lisa had an amazing ability to break a task down to small units and tackle it efficiently.

"Doc Tock," Lisa said, turning to her. "Could you show the team leaders—that's the first person I named for each team—where the cleaning supplies are?" Doc Tock was happy to do as she was asked.

Stevie, too, followed Lisa's directions. She'd been put on a team with Adam Levine and May Grover. Once again, she admired Lisa because she'd managed to balance each of the teams with older and younger kids, as well as mixing up boys and girls. She'd paid no attention to usual friendships. Though Stevie would have preferred to work with Lisa and Carole, it meant she was working with May, one of the younger riders who had a lot to learn, and Adam, who was taller and probably a little bit stronger than she was, and that mattered when they were working with the dogs in the big cages.

In fact, if she didn't like Lisa so much, she might envy her amazing skills.

"Oh, good," said Doc Tock, coming over to the cage of a

15

small mixed-breed dog that Stevie had just cleaned. May brought over a bowl of fresh water and Adam handed the pup a treat to chew on. "I need to take a blood sample from this fellow. Who wants to hold him?"

May offered first, so Stevie and Adam let her handle it. May opened the cage door and enticed the puppy to its entrance with a biscuit. The puppy came willingly, and May easily lifted him out and carried him to the table. She patted him gently, and the puppy settled in so happily with all the attention he was getting that he never seemed to notice what Doc Tock did to him.

Stevie got to hold the next dog—a medium-sized mutt of uncertain heritage—while he got his immunization, then Adam held a female named Daisy, who looked like a mix of retriever and shepherd, while Doc Tock examined her. Daisy was scheduled to be spayed in the next few days, and the vet needed to be sure she was in good health before she operated on her.

"She's a sweet dog," said Doc Tock, watching Daisy's tail swish eagerly. "I'm sure we'll find her a good home." Stevie found herself wishing that home could be hers, but she didn't think her cat, Madonna, would appreciate a big dog in the house. She didn't think her parents would appreciate it, either.

When Doc Tock was finished with the dogs, Stevie's

team joined another team that was painting some of the vacant cages so that they'd be ready for new occupants.

Carole, who had spent several vacations working as Judy Barker's assistant, was prepared to give Doc Tock a hand with anything. Together they took blood samples from several cats, set the deer's broken leg, and changed the bandage on a cat whose foot had been caught in a trap.

"All the cages are clean," Lisa reported to Doc Tock as she came out of the surgical room. "Everybody's been fed and watered, and ten cages have been painted."

"You guys are wonderful!" said the vet.

"What's next?" Lisa asked, still eager to help. Carole couldn't help noticing how Lisa had thrown herself into this whole project. Lisa was definitely good at organizing things, but she seemed to be in super mode today.

"Dr. Einstein," said Doc Tock.

"I thought he was dead," Lisa remarked.

"No, not the genius professor with the relativity theory. It's the owl in the corner over there with the broken foot," Doc Tock told her. "He won't let anybody near him, and he won't eat anything. I'm afraid we're going to lose him. You've already worked a couple of miracles here today. Want to try for another?"

Lisa blushed. "I don't know about that," she said. "But I'll try."

Carole looked over to where the owl was cowering in the corner of his cage, sitting awkwardly on the ground while he protected his wounded foot.

Lisa picked up a bowl of fresh meat and a toothpick and approached the cage cautiously. She pulled a stool along with her and sat down on it. Then she looked into the cage and began talking gently. Carole tried to hear what she was saying, but she knew the words wouldn't make any difference. What was important was the sound of Lisa's voice. There were a few voices outside the room, but in the cage room, nobody spoke except Lisa.

She looked sideways into the cage, keeping her eyes from looking directly into the owl's, which might be perceived as a challenge, a dare. She saw when the owl looked at her and then averted her eyes completely, showing submission.

The riders had all learned about this kind of communication with animals when they'd studied horse training techniques. To animals, it was important who was dominating and who was submitting. If Lisa remained submissive, the owl would feel it had nothing to fear from her.

The owl took one step forward along the side of the cage. Lisa remained still. The owl took a second step. Very slowly, very smoothly, Lisa took a bit of the meat and put it on the toothpick, holding it within Dr. Einstein's field of vision but not moving it toward him.

The owl watched; he didn't blink.

He took another step toward Lisa.

Lisa moved the meat toward the bird. Dr. Einstein stepped back.

Lisa withdrew the meat. Dr. Einstein stepped forward.

Carole held her breath.

For fifteen minutes, Lisa and Dr. Einstein continued their little dance, Lisa approaching, the bird withdrawing, and then vice versa. Each time, though, Lisa let the bit of meat on the stick stay just a little bit closer to the bird, and each time he withdrew a little less. Finally the meat was inside the bars of the cage, and Lisa was absolutely still, gazing at the floor. The bird only had eyes for the meat.

When it happened, it was so fast that most of the students missed it altogether, but Carole was glad she hadn't blinked. The bird snatched the piece of meat from the toothpick and swallowed it, and Lisa was left with an empty toothpick. Slowly she replenished the supply and the dance began again. Only this time it didn't take so long. Dr. Einstein had been building up a serious hunger since he'd arrived at CARL the week before, and he was ready to eat. Four more times, he took meat from the toothpick.

Lisa stood up and walked slowly over to the group of watching students. Doc Tock gave her a hug.

"That was great!" she said. Lisa beamed. "You're saving the life of a great horned owl—something nobody else could do. You're amazing!"

The students patted her on the back and Carole hugged her as well. "Fantastic," she told her friend. Lisa could barely speak.

"Okay, guys," Max said, calling for their attention. "I think our work here is done for a while. As you know, all of you are welcome to volunteer here at any time. Of course, that will cut into your stable chores, and knowing how you feel about mucking out stalls, I'm sure Doc Tock won't be able to draw you away."

The students laughed. Mucking out stalls was just one of the jobs all of them had to do at Pine Hollow. Max liked to emphasize that there was much more to horses than riding. He also liked to point out that helping with chores kept the costs down at his stable, so most of the students were willing to pitch in.

"Don't worry, Doc," Stevie said. "We'll be able to pull ourselves away from the manure pile and give you a hand every once in a while."

"That's all I'll need," said the veterinarian. "Thank you all for your help this morning. I hope I'll see you again soon."

"May I stay?" Lisa asked, speaking to nobody in particular and everybody in general.

"You want to help out some more?" Doc Tock asked.

Lisa nodded. The vet looked at Max.

"You'd be missing the lesson," he reminded her.

"It's okay."

"As long as you call your parents," Max said.

"I will," Lisa promised. "But they won't have to pick me up. I can walk home."

"You're going to Stevie's," Carole reminded her.

"I can walk there, too," said Lisa.

"Are you sure?" Stevie asked. It was hard to imagine anyone wanting to miss a riding class.

"I want to help with the raccoon," she said, looking to Doc Tock for permission.

"It's fine by me," she said. "I can always use help."

"We'll see you at Stevie's, then," Carole said.

"Bye," Lisa said, turning toward the cages.

Carole and Stevie walked back to Pine Hollow together, but Carole wasn't in a talking mood. She was more in a thinking mood. She remembered Lisa's weird morning—or, more accurately, Mr. and Mrs. Atwood's weird

21

morning, and then how Lisa had seemed to turn into Super Girl and now wanted to skip the riding lesson. She guessed that if Lisa had found something she really wanted to do more than having a riding lesson, it was probably good for her. Besides, they'd have a chance to talk that night at Stevie's.

LISA SIGHED. HER work was finished for the day. She'd
helped Doc Tock stitch a gash on the raccoon's belly, and
she'd talked to three people interested in adopting puppies. She'd even had the pleasure of helping one little boy
choose a cat.

The day was over and it was time to meet her friends at
Stevie's. She thanked Doc Tock for letting her stay and
work.

"I'm the one who's thankful," the vet told her, shooing
her out the door. "Now go have fun!"

It was hard to imagine having more fun than she'd just
had, helping both animals and people. When she stopped
to think about it, though, she realized that spending the

night at Stevie's might be more fun. Being with her friends was always great.

She'd left her riding clothes at Pine Hollow. That was fine. They were clean and they'd be in her cubby waiting for her in the morning. What she'd forgotten, however, was to bring her overnight things from home. It was unlike her to be forgetful, but she recalled that she and Carole had been a little rushed, wanting to be sure not to be late to the stable that morning. Anyway, it was no big deal. She could stop off at home and pick up her pajamas, clean clothes, and toothbrush since her house was right down the block from Stevie's.

She looked at her watch, knowing her friends would have finished their lesson and their ride by now and would be preparing to get to Stevie's fairly soon. Everything would work smoothly. Lisa would even have time to tell her parents all about her day at CARL.

She cringed. She'd forgotten to call them, even though she'd promised Max she would. She should have done it, she knew. Her parents needed to know where she was. She was sure they wouldn't mind, but it was her responsibility to let them know. That was two things she'd forgotten that day. Was there anything else? She hoped not.

Mrs. Atwood was in the kitchen when Lisa came in. Lisa went over and gave her a hug, and Mrs. Atwood wrinkled her nose.

"I guess I smell, huh?" Lisa said. "It couldn't be helped, though, and wait until I tell you what I've been doing!"

"Why don't you shower first?" Mrs. Atwood said. Lisa thought maybe that would be a good idea. She ran upstairs, showered and changed, put what she needed for the night into a backpack, and was back downstairs in less than fifteen minutes.

"Where's Dad?" Lisa asked. She'd noticed that both cars were in the driveway. Normally her father would have come to greet her.

"I don't know," said Mrs. Atwood.

Lisa poured herself a glass of milk and got some graham crackers from the cabinet. She settled down at the kitchen table, where her mother was sitting with a cup of coffee. On the counter, the television was showing a golf tournament. Mrs. Atwood stared at the screen. Lisa couldn't ever remember her mother watching golf before. She dunked a cracker into the milk and took a bite. Her mother didn't say anything.

"I had the greatest day, Mom," Lisa began.

"Good," said her mother.

"Well, I should have called you, I guess, but I got so involved . . ."

Lisa told her mother all about her day at CARL, about organizing the teams and cleaning the cages. She told her about feeding Dr. Einstein.

"And when he finally took the meat—well, you wouldn't believe how exciting it was," she said. "Nobody in the whole place said a word until I got him to take the fourth bite. Isn't that great?"

"Yes, of course. You're good with horses," her mother said.

"It's a bird," she reminded her mother. "A great horned owl."

"Oh," said her mother. "What do you want for dinner?"

"I'm going over to Stevie's," Lisa said.

Mrs. Atwood looked at her watch. "What time are you due?"

"Whenever I get there," Lisa said. "Like about now."

"Good night, darling. I'll see you tomorrow afternoon, after riding, then, right?"

"Right," Lisa said, kissing her mother.

She picked up her overnight bag and walked into the hallway toward the front door. As she passed the den, she saw that her father was there. He'd apparently finished his paper, because he was now reading a magazine.

"Good night, Dad," she said.

He glanced at his watch. "Isn't it a little early for bed?" he asked.

Lisa laughed. "I'm going over to Stevie's."

"Oh, well, then, good night," he said, blowing her a kiss.

Lisa slung her bag over her shoulder and paused before leaving.

"I saved an animal's life today," she said.

"Good," said her dad, looking up from his magazine.

"It was an owl."

"They eat rodents," said her father.

"This one ate steak," she told him.

"Good," he said, turning his attention back to his magazine. "Right, well, good night."

"Night," she said. She left him flipping the pages.

It was a short walk over to Stevie's. Lisa drew her sweater around her shoulders against the cool night air. She wasn't sorry she'd forgotten her bag at home. She was glad she'd gotten to tell her parents a little bit about her work at CARL. They weren't always interested in her schoolwork or her riding, but they'd seemed proud of the volunteer work she was doing at CARL. It was a place where she felt she could make a difference.

Lisa could almost hear Stevie's house before she saw it.

It was nearly dark and a few lights had been turned on in the house, but through the open windows the chaotic sounds of the Lake family carried into the neighborhood.

"I did not!" It was Chad's voice. He was fourteen and his voice had changed. It fairly boomed.

"You're always saying that to me!" said another voice Lisa recognized as Alex's. Although the greatest rivalries were between Stevie and her brothers, these days Alex seemed to be more and more willing to challenge Chad's position as king of the hill.

"I say it because I'm right!" yelled Chad.

"Upstairs, both of you!" Mr. Lake called out. "Work it out between the two of you and work it out quietly!"

Lisa could even hear the thumps of the two teenage boys' oversized feet as they chased each other up the stairs.

Lisa neared the front door.

"Mom, if they're sent away from the table tonight, can I have Alex's dessert?" That was Michael. He sometimes seemed angelic, but he didn't fool anybody for long, especially not his mother.

"You'd better go upstairs, too," said Mrs. Lake. "Your father and I need a few minutes of peace and quiet."

"What did I do wrong?" Michael asked.

As Lisa knocked and entered, she saw Mrs. Lake in the kitchen.

28

"It isn't what you did," Mrs. Lake said, putting her hands on her hips and smiling. "It's what you're thinking about doing."

Michael sighed. "I can't get away with anything," he said.

"You've got that right!" declared Mrs. Lake. She laughed, and so did Michael. Whatever he'd been up to, it had been nipped in the bud.

"Oh, hi, Lisa," Mrs. Lake said, noticing her arrival. She removed her oven mitts and tossed them on the kitchen counter, then led Lisa toward the den.

"Hi, Mr. Lake. Are Stevie and Carole here yet?"

"They are," answered Mr. Lake from the sofa, where he was watching the same golf tournament Lisa's mother had been staring at a few minutes earlier. "I think I heard them expressing some intention of talking about—what is it you girls like so much? Is it camels?" He was teasing and Lisa knew it.

"No sir," she said. "We're zebra fans. Why can't you remember?"

"You'd think I'd remember after all this time!" he said. "Oh, will you look at that putt?"

Lisa looked. It seemed that the ball made an S-curve on the green before dropping into the cup. It was pretty amazing.

29

"Well, go on up, then. They're definitely going to want to hear your opinion about, uh, uh, those giraffes."

"Bullfighting," Lisa corrected him.

"*Olé!*"

"Tell Stevie and Carole dinner will be ready in about half an hour," Mrs. Lake said. "And if you see any of our sons, you can give them the same message."

"Will do," Lisa said.

Mrs. Lake plopped down on the sofa next to her husband, took his hand, and looked at the television. "Now who's in the lead?" she asked.

"The guy in the funny hat," said Mr. Lake.

The door to Stevie's room was closed against the clamor that filled the hallway, caused by her brothers' battalions of jettisoned stuffed animals.

"Time!" Lisa called, ducking under a flying teddy bear. There was a brief but noticeable truce while she made her way into Stevie's room. She knew the truce was over by the thud on Stevie's door as soon as it closed behind her.

"You made it safely through enemy territory?" Stevie asked.

"Barely," Lisa said, slipping her bag off her shoulder and sinking onto the floor. Stevie and Carole each tossed her a pillow for comfort.

"Well, how was it after we left?" Stevie asked.

"Awesome," said Lisa. "I had a great time working with Doc Tock. That place is wonderful. It's like everybody knows there's work to be done; they all do it and nobody complains because everyone knows it's got to be done and it makes a difference. You should have seen the kid who came to pick out a cat. It was like love at first sight."

"Which cat did he choose?" Carole asked. She'd seen almost all the animals while making the rounds with Doc Tock.

"The calico," said Lisa. "She's still a kitten, and when their eyes met—well, you just knew it was forever."

"I wish I'd been there," said Carole.

"Right, like you'd miss a lesson and a hack for all the tea in China," Stevie said.

"Horses aren't the only animals I love," Carole retorted.

"But they're the ones you love best," Stevie reminded her.

"No argument," Carole agreed. "Well, if I couldn't be there, I'm glad you were."

"My parents thought it was great," Lisa said. "I stopped at home to pick up my stuff on the way here. I told them all about it."

"Of course they thought it was great," said Stevie. "You're their daughter—their only child living at home. Everything you do is great."

31

"Sort of," Lisa said. "But anyway, I'm going to go back to CARL every day."

"Every day?" said Stevie. "But what about Pine Hollow?"

"What about horses?" Carole asked.

"Don't worry," Lisa said. "I'll get to Pine Hollow. I love horses, too, you know."

"But there's so much to do at CARL," Stevie protested.

"That's the point, isn't it?"

"You'll end up spending all your time there," Stevie said.

"No, I can do both. I love both places, I'll get to both places. You can love two places at once, can't you?"

"I guess," said Carole, but in truth she wasn't at all sure she could ever love any place as much as she loved a stable, any stable, and there was no way she'd ever love any stable as much as she loved Pine Hollow.

"Don't worry. You'll see plenty of me at Pine Hollow," Lisa told her friends.

Assured, they turned their talk to horses until the call came up that dinner was ready. Dinner at the Lakes' was as rambunctious a time as any other. There was a constant threat of food fights. Mr. and Mrs. Lake seemed, to Lisa, to alternate between bemusement and genuine concern for the future of the fruit salad. During everyone's third helping of pasta, Lisa realized she was really exhausted from her long day. Caring for animals was draining, and she didn't have the energy to worry about flying melon balls.

After dinner and cleanup, the girls retreated to Stevie's room. Lisa won the toss for the cot. She donned her pajamas, unfolded the bed, and put Stevie's sleeping bag on it. She shimmied into it and rested her head on the pillow.

Right next to her, Stevie and Carole were having an animated conversation that centered around Joe Novick's inability to keep his heels down, even though he'd been riding much longer than Lisa, and how Patch must get tired of having his rider unbalanced that way.

Lisa's mind wandered. There was vigorous activity going on in the hallway, a continuation of the stuffed animal battle that had begun before dinner. Downstairs, Mr. and Mrs. Lake were playing a contentious game of backgammon. Lisa had seen them at it before. They bet when they played backgammon—a full thousand dollars a game. Lisa had seen the score pad, too. They had a running total that they'd been keeping since before their children were born. Sometimes they were pretty even. The last time Lisa had seen it, Mrs. Lake had been up ninety-eight thousand dollars, but from the sound of Mr. Lake's victorious cries, the score had evened out considerably that night.

There was noise everywhere in this house. People

argued, threatened, competed. It was very different from Lisa's house. Things were almost always quiet at the Atwoods'. But even all the noise wasn't going to keep Lisa awake that night. She slipped into a dreamless sleep while Carole and Stevie compared the jumping styles of Belle and Starlight, a subject that could keep them talking all night long.

LISA WINCED. No matter how much she cared about the animals at CARL, and no matter how important she knew the work was, it still didn't make the litter boxes smell any better. But they had to be cleaned, so she was doing it.

"You're tireless!" Anita, the receptionist, told her.

"Not really," said Lisa. "I mean, I don't get tired because I know that what I'm doing is important."

"I think you're the first volunteer we've ever had who thought cleaning litter boxes was important."

"I didn't say it was fun," said Lisa.

"Yes, at least you didn't say that!" Anita teased. "And when you're done, I've got a treat for you."

"What?"

"Well, there's a new puppy that came in and he needs to be taken for a walk."

"I'm your woman!" Lisa said. One of the things she enjoyed most was taking the dogs for walks. The dogs spent a good part of the day in their cages, so they all liked to get out, and it was good for them. It was especially important for the puppies, who needed to learn to be walked on a leash.

As quickly as she could, Lisa finished cleaning the litter box and then took Anita up on her offer of walking the puppy. As soon as she clipped the lead on the yellow curly-haired pup's collar, he started leaping with excitement. Lisa knew he'd been abandoned and wondered how he'd learned so quickly to love leashes. Perhaps it was in the genes, or maybe another dog at CARL had told him about it.

He leaped happily as they left the building, and he continued to jump with excitement for their promenade on the sidewalk. He paid no attention whatsoever to any instructions Lisa tried to give him about proper walking manners, but they both had fun.

When their fifteen minutes were up, it took a lot of work on Lisa's part to convince the puppy to turn around and go back. Lisa was glad he was still pretty small. She just picked him up and turned him in the right direction. That seemed to change the dog's mind. He began jumping toward his temporary home instead of away from it. Lisa laughed at his eagerness.

A truck pulled into CARL's driveway in front of Lisa and the puppy. It was a truck Lisa knew well because it belonged to Judy Barker, Pine Hollow's vet. That was odd, because there were no horses at CARL, and horses were Judy's specialty. She'd help out with the small animals or fill in for Doc Tock in an emergency, but as of the last fifteen minutes there were neither any horses nor any emergencies at CARL.

The puppy was getting stubborn again, perhaps sensing that his freedom was about to be curtailed. Lisa bent down and picked him up. At first he wiggled against her grasp, but as she began to stroke and scratch him gently, he gave up resistance and simply enjoyed the attention. He was practically purring by the time she slipped him back into his cage.

"What are you doing here?" Lisa asked Judy. "We don't have any horses in residence."

"I could ask you the same thing," Judy said. "I was just at Pine Hollow and your friends are taking a jumping class. Shouldn't you be with them?"

"I decided to spend a little time helping out here this afternoon," Lisa explained.

37

"And yesterday afternoon and the two days before that," Anita said. "She's becoming a permanent fixture—and a welcome one at that!"

"Thanks," Lisa said. "I'm mostly having fun with the small animals."

"Well, now you're about to start having fun with a horse," Judy said. "Angus Rutherford found a stray horse hanging around at the back of his pasture. It was frightening his cattle, so he called me and I told him to bring the fellow over here."

As if on cue, a large farmer's truck with a horse trailer in tow pulled into CARL's drive and slowed to a stop.

"Can you give me a hand, Lisa?" Judy asked. "I have the feeling this guy's not going to be too enthusiastic about backing down the ramp."

Lisa went to the back of the truck and unlatched the door. What she saw inside was a dirty, scraggly, skinny horse, and she felt a catch in her throat.

"Oh," she said.

"Don't worry," Judy told her. "We'll look after this fellow, won't we?"

They opened the doors completely, and while Judy slid the ramp out of the back of the trailer, Lisa climbed in to take a closer look at CARL's newest resident. At first she thought he was mostly mud-colored, but on second look she realized that what she was seeing *was* mud—and scabs. The horse had a lot of cuts, and his coat was a mess. His mane and tail seemed hopelessly tangled. His ears flattened against his head, indicating that he wasn't in a mood to trust anyone. Even in the dim light of the trailer, Lisa could see plenty of signs of infestation. It turned her stomach to think how many ticks they were going to find on him.

"It's okay, boy," she said, automatically falling into her habit of talking in a calm voice to an unfamiliar animal. "I think you're going to like it here, because everybody here is going to like you." She kept talking and didn't make any sudden moves until she saw his ears begin to perk up. Then she reached for him slowly and gave him a little pat on his cheek—a place she'd learned most horses find irresistible. It was a good time to give him a treat, but she hadn't brought any carrots, apple, or sugar with her. She felt around in her jacket pocket and pulled out a piece of her peanut butter and jelly sandwich left over from lunch. It was mashed and unappetizing to her, but it just might be the treat this horse had been dreaming about. She took the mangled mass out of its plastic bag and held it out for the horse's inspection.

He sniffed once and then he took it. The sandwich morsel was gone in a flash. The horse's ears perked up brightly and he looked straight into Lisa's eyes. The look said only one thing: More!

Lisa burst out laughing. She patted him again, took hold of his old and very worn halter, clipped a lead line on it, and then began bringing him out of the trailer. He seemed uncertain until Lisa realized that he was lame in one leg and probably hurting in all the others, to say nothing of the rest of him. This was a sick horse that needed a lot of help. But sick as he was, he willingly followed the source of peanut butter and jelly sandwich out of the trailer and onto solid ground.

"Good job!" said Judy. "What's your secret?"

"If I told you, it wouldn't be a secret," Lisa joked. "Anyway, this guy and I have found the basis of a beautiful friendship. In his case, it's food."

"Not surprising," said Judy. "Just look at those ribs."

Lisa did and then was sorry she had. In the daylight the horse looked even worse than he had in the dim light of the trailer. She knew that a lot of what looked awful was just superficial—things like mud and scratches. Other things would take longer to fix, and Lisa was glad that Judy would be the one looking after those.

"Put him in the paddock, will you?" Judy asked.

Because CARL was a temporary shelter, it didn't have a real barn. What it could offer a visiting horse was a small paddock with a covered area where the horse could go for protection from bad weather.

The fact that this horse was wearing a halter meant he had once belonged to someone and had somehow gotten separated from his owner. He had managed to survive in the wild on his own, but the sight of a paddock with a fence, with the promise of plentiful fresh water and the smell of clean hay, lifted his spirits visibly. Lisa let him loose in the little paddock, and he went right over to the water bucket. No surprise after a peanut butter and jelly sandwich, Lisa joked to herself. Too bad she didn't have some milk for him!

Once the horse had had some feed and a good long drink of water, Judy began her examination. Lisa helped, as she often did when Judy examined the horses at Pine Hollow. Judy checked the horse's vital signs: his temperature, heart rate, and breathing. All were normal, and that was really good news. If a horse had a bad internal infection or a disease, its vital signs would be out of whack. The fact that they were normal was the first sure sign that this horse was going to be all right.

Judy asked Lisa to get a bandage to wrap the swollen leg. Even though Judy hadn't examined it carefully yet, Lisa knew that it was going to need to be wrapped. She turned and walked quickly in the direction of the main building.

"Ouch!" Judy yipped.

"What was that?" Lisa asked, turning around.

41

Judy had backed away from the horse and was looking a little annoyed at him.

"Not so friendly after all," she said. "He just kicked me." She rubbed her shin. "Not that it's the first time a horse has kicked me, but this guy seemed pretty cooperative."

"Want me to stay?"

"No, I'll be okay. I have to do this myself," Judy said. Lisa suspected that was a veterinarian's equivalent of getting back on the horse after being thrown. For riders, that was a way of overcoming their fear by facing it.

Lisa paused to watch, wanting to be sure the horse and vet were both okay. As soon as Judy reached toward the horse's head, Lisa could see his leg muscles tense up. He was going to kick again. Judy saw it, too, and withdrew her hand.

"He was okay until you started to leave," Judy said to Lisa.

"Well, I didn't prod him with any instruments," she said jokingly.

"Make me the bad guy, huh?" Judy retorted.

"I think I've got an idea," Lisa told her. "Wait just a minute."

She hurried into the main building, where there was a whole shelf stocked with animal treats. She found a small

42

supply of carrots—most of them had already been eaten by the raccoon—and an apple.

She brought them out, along with the leg bandage, and stayed by the horse's head, giving him occasional treats while Judy examined every inch of him and took blood samples.

When she was done, Judy gave the horse a pat. He almost nipped her, but Lisa got a carrot into his mouth in the nick of time.

"He's not well-mannered," said Judy. "And while I'm glad to have you save me from a feisty horse, it's not really a good idea to give him treats while he's behaving badly. It's like you're rewarding the bad behavior."

"It's his first day here and he must be scared to death," Lisa said.

"You're right, but be careful around him. I don't think you should groom him."

That was just what Lisa had been planning to do next. "He's going to feel much better when he's clean," she pleaded.

"And I'm going to feel better if you don't end up in the hospital," said Judy.

"Okay, but at least let me give it a try. You can give him treats for a few minutes while I groom him."

Judy sighed. "Okay," she said. "We'll just see how he be-haves. The first kick and we're both out of here."

Lisa didn't wait for Judy to have second thoughts. She hurried over to the storage area where she knew the horse equipment was kept and brought back a grooming bucket. The horse didn't want Judy to hold his halter. He made that very clear. But he didn't mind when Lisa clipped the lead line back on and gave that to the vet.

He watched suspiciously when Lisa put the bucket down nearby. His ears went back on his head.

"Lisa . . . ," Judy began.

"I'm okay," she said. And then she began talking to the horse again. She showed him the soft brush she was going to begin with and let him sniff it. She even let him take a little bite at it. She could tell it didn't taste good; the dis-appointment was visible in his look. The horse must have figured out it was harmless and, Lisa thought, he probably recognized it.

Gently she began stroking his coat, beginning with the dried mud. It was painstaking work because there were so many cuts and scrapes that it would have been easy for her to hurt him unintentionally. Whenever she recognized a raw spot, she simply brushed around it. There would be plenty of time in the future to get him really clean. For now, superficial would do.

44

"You're amazing," said Judy, speaking quietly. "Doc Tock told me what you did with the owl the other day, and now he's healthy and quite tame. It's like you can speak to them."

"I learned a lot of this from you," Lisa said as she continued working.

"Well, I must be a better teacher than I realized," Judy said.

"The owl was just luck," Lisa said. "And patience. This guy and I have a real bond, though."

"That secret?" Judy asked.

"I guess," said Lisa. She stood back and took a look at what she'd accomplished so far. She was surprised to discover that in spite of the mud, the cuts, and the visible ribs, she was working on a rather handsome horse. He was a light chestnut with a blaze and white socks on three legs. It might be socks on four legs, but there was still too much dirt on one of his ankles to be sure. The light color was very distinct, and it made Lisa smile.

"He needs a name," she said.

"And I suppose you have something in mind?" Judy asked.

"I do."

"Is that a secret, too?" asked the vet.

"No, it *is* the secret," said Lisa. "I hereby dub him Peanut Butter and Jelly—PJ for short."

Judy laughed. "I guess I know how you tamed this wild beast then, don't I?"

"Yep. And I know it's not very good for him except in small amounts."

"Like leftover sandwich pieces?" Judy asked.

"Just like that," Lisa confirmed.

She picked up the brush and went back to work. PJ behaved like a perfect gentleman, even when Judy let go of the lead rope.

LISA WAS LATE getting home. She was afraid her mother would be worried about her, but there had been so much to do! Once she'd finished getting the worst of the mud off PJ, she'd helped Anita take a picture of him, which they'd use for posters, and then they'd called a couple of the local papers to place ads about the lost horse. Finally, working with a list Judy gave her, she called all the equine vets in nearby counties. Somebody had to know about a missing horse.

It was hard work taking care of a horse who was as ill, sore, and distrustful as this one. Her day had involved lots of patience and concentration, and it was all Lisa could do to keep from yawning as she hurried home. She couldn't wait to tell her parents.

She eagerly hurried up the steps to the kitchen door. What she found inside, however, was not her mother, but a note: "Your father is working late again. I'm at an appointment. There are leftovers. Love, Mom."

So much for the nice conversation she'd been looking forward to having. Lisa put her book bag in her room, changed into clean clothes, and went back downstairs to see what her mother's idea of leftovers was. She couldn't remember what they'd had for dinner the night before. Hadn't that been leftovers? She pulled open the refrigerator door and peered inside. There were a number of plastic containers and bowls. Their contents revealed fried chicken, corn, and french fries. She made a plate and put it in the microwave. Setting the timer, she went up to her room to get her history book so that she could read while she ate. It was going to be hard to stay awake long enough to get her homework done, so she figured she'd better get started.

Four minutes later, the electronic beep told her that dinner was heated. When she returned to the kitchen, she realized that it was actually a good deal more than heated. Still hopeful, she poked the chicken with a fork. It looked a little bit like chicken, but it felt more like shoe leather. The fries, instead of being crispy, were mushy and unappetizing.

48

"I guess I've got some more work to do on microwaving," she said to her dog, Dolly, who watched all the proceedings. She even looked hopefully at the dish.

"No way," Lisa told her. "I can't give this to you. There are laws about cruelty to animals!" The little dog retreated and took a drink from her water bowl.

Lisa tossed the food into the garbage and thought about what she might be able to eat that she couldn't ruin. She took out the bread, peanut butter, and jelly and poured herself a big glass of cold milk.

With the first bite, she was overwhelmed with sweet memories of her afternoon working with PJ. She couldn't wait to tell her friends all about CARL's newest resident.

As if on cue, the phone rang. It was Stevie and Carole on a three-way call.

"Are we interrupting dinner?" Carole asked.

"I'm not sure if what I'm eating qualifies as dinner," Lisa said, looking down at the remains of her sandwich. "But I'm alone, so I can talk."

"Good," said Stevie. "Because we haven't talked anywhere near enough in days! Where have you been?"

"I've been at CARL," Lisa said.

"You've missed two riding lessons," Carole reminded her.

"I know, but these guys need me—and I'm having fun."

"Right, like cleaning out litter boxes is fun!"

It hurt a little when Stevie said that. It wasn't as if there was any glamour to the work Lisa was doing, but the boxes needed to be cleaned out. Why couldn't Stevie understand that?

"Are you ever coming back to Pine Hollow?" Carole asked. Lisa could tell she was asking the question that really concerned her and Stevie. It surprised her that the subject even came up between them.

"Of course I am!" she said. "I just feel like right now this is really important."

"We didn't mean to say it wasn't," Stevie said, clearly pulling back. "We know it's important. We miss you, though."

"And so does Prancer," Carole added. "There's always plenty of work to do at Pine Hollow."

"Oh, I know that," said Lisa. "And speaking of horses, Judy brought a stray over to CARL today. I guess he had been hanging around on the edge of a farmer's field for a while until the guy could catch him. It's a light chestnut gelding. He was probably nice-looking before he got lost, but now he's skinny, scratched up, and really dirty. He made friends with me okay, but he kicked Judy a couple of times."

That got her friends' interest. They wanted to know all about PJ and loved the story about the sandwich.

"You're turning into some sort of miracle worker with stray animals," said Carole, recalling Lisa's job with Dr. Einstein.

"Oh, I don't know about that," Lisa said. "It's just that I feel so sorry for them, it's like I understand what's in their heads."

"Well, what else is going on?" Stevie asked.

"I guess that's about it at CARL," Lisa said.

"No, I meant anything else anywhere else? It's like we haven't talked in weeks."

"Days," Lisa reminded her. "Nothing too interesting. I've got a history quiz tomorrow."

"Spellbinding," Stevie joked.

"Another A for you," said Carole.

"Not if I don't study before I fall asleep. I'm really tired," said Lisa. "And I have to be at CARL tomorrow afternoon. Judy's getting back some of the blood test results on PJ—that's what I've named him, after the sandwich, you know—and I want to be sure he's okay."

"Sure," said Carole. "Tell you what. Stevie and I will meet you there after school and help you with PJ and the other animals, and then we can all go to Pine Hollow together, okay?"

"Okay," said Lisa. "I can't wait for you to meet this guy. He's wonderful."

51

"No point in telling Carole that," Stevie said. "She thinks all horses are wonderful."

"And am I ever wrong?" Carole asked.

"Spoken like a true Saddle Club member!" said Stevie.

"I'll see you guys tomorrow," Lisa said. "And thanks for calling."

As she hung up the phone, she had the distinct feeling that she'd just been on the receiving end of a Saddle Club project. Her friends were worried about her or else they wouldn't have insisted on meeting her at CARL tomorrow. They didn't have anything to worry about, though. Lisa was fine. It was PJ who needed help. He would be the next Saddle Club project.

Lisa finished the last bite of her sandwich, put her dishes in the dishwasher, grabbed an apple for dessert, and headed upstairs to finish her homework. She had a lot of things going on. She was working hard at school. She didn't want to run the risk of letting her grades slip, because that would really disappoint her parents. And then there was all her work at CARL. Her parents had seemed pleased to hear about that. They were proud of her, and she wanted to make them happy.

She plopped onto her bed and pulled her history textbook toward her. Now, where was Julius Caesar the last time she looked? Right. He was conquering Gaul. She took a bite of her apple and turned her attention to the battles in Switzerland—then known as Helvetia.

Lisa's mother called about eight o'clock to make sure she was okay, and Lisa assured her that she was. Mrs. Atwood said she'd be home later, and Lisa told her she'd see her then. There was so much to tell her. Her mother said she hoped they'd have time to talk soon. She had a lot going on, too, but she was calling from a borrowed cell phone in a restaurant and she really couldn't talk just then.

"I just wanted to be sure you're okay."

"I am, Mom. Good night."

Ten minutes later, she got a similar call from her father, which was a surprise, because she'd thought her parents were at the restaurant together.

"Sorry not to be there tonight," her father said.

"I don't mind," Lisa assured him. "I'm studying for a test. But I've got lots of stuff I want to tell you about."

"Well, now you have to study, I guess. I love you, Lisa," he said.

"Love you, too, Dad. Good night."

She was glad of the quiet, and now it was time to get back to Caesar.

THE NEXT MORNING Lisa woke up at dawn. Her room was gray in the early morning light, and the house was as quiet as it had been the night before. The only noise was Dolly, who was sleeping on the foot of her bed, snoring gently. As soon as Lisa sat up, Dolly awakened.

She looked at her watch. It was 6:15. She didn't have to be at school until eight. If she hurried, she could stop by CARL on her way to school and check on PJ. Her parents wouldn't be up for another half hour. It would mean she'd miss them, but PJ was important, and she was sure they'd understand.

She hurried through her morning routine, then picked up her book bag and went downstairs. In the kitchen she made two peanut butter and jelly sandwiches—one for herself and one for PJ—and grabbed a couple of apples and two containers of milk. She scribbled a note for her mother and headed for the front door. As she passed the den, she noticed a pile of blankets on the sofa, and then realized it wasn't really a pile of blankets. It was her father with some blankets on him. He must have gotten in really late the night before and hadn't wanted to wake up Lisa's mother. She blew him a silent kiss and went out the front door.

Lisa loved this time of day. The air was fresh and cool— so different from inside the house. She took a deep breath and exhaled, feeling invigorated. There were stirrings in some of the neighbors' houses, but it was earlier than most people were up, so it felt like the whole world was hers alone. She reached out her hands as if to hug the air and everything else. There was a skip in her walk. She couldn't help feeling that way. Life was good, wasn't it?

She paused at a stone wall near CARL to retie a loose shoelace. She was thinking about her parents, realizing that it had been so long since they'd all been together that she might forget some of the things she wanted to tell them. It wasn't like she needed to boast to them. It was just that they always seemed to get such pleasure from knowing about the good things she was doing, things that made a difference, and she didn't want to deny them that pleasure. Yes, that was it. She wanted to do that nice thing for them. She took out her assignment notebook and turned to a blank page at the back. She made a few notes to herself.

Dinner tonight, she thought. *That's when we'll all have a chance to talk.*

She stood up and picked up her backpack. She could practically hear PJ calling her name.

6

LISA LET HERSELF into PJ's paddock. The horse was standing motionless in the small shelter. Lisa approached him, speaking gently. His ears perked.

"You were waiting for me, weren't you, boy?" she asked. He didn't answer.

She patted him cautiously, still very aware of his wounds and tender spots. He flinched when she accidentally touched a sore spot, but he never threatened her as he had Judy.

"You're really a tame old boy, aren't you?" she asked. He didn't answer that question, either, but Lisa was confident she had the answer anyway.

She looked again at his scratches. She could see several

that formed a distinct pattern of parallel lines. Judy said it looked as if he'd tangled with a bobcat, and it looked to Lisa as if the bobcat had nearly won. Perhaps that was when PJ had learned to kick so effectively. It was a skill Lisa hoped he would soon forget.

She took the salve off the shelf in the shed and gently put some on each of his scratches to help the healing process. She noticed there was one in particular that seemed swollen, and he didn't want her to touch it. She took a piece of paper out of her backpack and scribbled a note for Judy. The flesh around that scratch was warm, indicating that PJ might be developing an infection in that wound. Judy might want to give him some antibiotics just to be sure.

"Good boy," she said, patting him carefully. This time he answered with an affectionate flick of his tail. Lisa's heart nearly burst with joy. It was a small thing, but from PJ it was really a big deal. He was definitely feeling better, and he wanted her to know it.

She replenished his water bucket and gave him some fresh hay. While he busied himself with his water and snack, she took up the soft brush and again attempted to groom him very gently. Although he was getting cleaner, Lisa found herself thinking that the brushing was more exploratory than anything else, because every time she brushed his coat she found another wound.

When she looked at her watch and saw it was almost eight, she knew she had to leave. PJ whinnied and then nickered as Lisa headed for the gate. She turned around and he nickered again, looking her straight in the eye. It was as if he were trying to say something to her, as if he didn't want her to go.

"I can't stay, PJ. I've got to get to school." She hoped he would understand. She turned and he whinnied. What was on his mind?

Then Lisa laughed. She remembered exactly what was on his mind, and if it weren't for his really good sense of smell, he might not have known to ask for it. He simply wanted his sandwich!

"Okay, okay, you win!" she said, reaching into her backpack. "Half now, half later. But you'll only get the second half if I hear that you were on your best behavior for Judy's visit this afternoon!"

She tore off a bit of the sandwich and gave it to him. He chomped very contentedly on his morning treat. To top it off, she gave him a slug of milk from a half-pint container. He positively guzzled the milk, proving that milk is the best accompaniment for a peanut butter and jelly sandwich. He made a mess of it, though. Milk cartons had not been designed for horses' drinking habits.

Lisa checked her watch again, then hurried out the

gate. She had just ten minutes to get to school, and it was a fifteen-minute walk.

"WHERE'S LISA?" STEVIE asked Carole. The two of them had agreed to meet at CARL after school so that they would at least have a chance to see their friend. Now they were there and Stevie wondered where she was.

"She had to stay after school because she was late this morning. A half hour of detention," said Carole.

"Late?" Stevie asked. It was very unlike Lisa to be late for anything, ever.

"She told me she came over here this morning and just couldn't pull herself away from PJ. Anyway, she'll be here in a few minutes, and I'm kind of glad you and I have a chance to talk before she gets here. She's been acting really strange."

"Surely you're not saying that just because she's crazy about this horse, are you?"

Carole smiled. "No there's nothing strange about that. It's the way she's so focused on this project. And the fact that she hasn't been over to Pine Hollow."

"Well, at least now we get to meet this horse that she's so crazy about," Stevie said.

The two girls went into the main building of CARL together and signed the volunteer log. They left their book bags and jackets in the cloakroom, then went out the back door to the paddock to meet PJ.

They found the horse standing in the shade of a tree in the corner of the paddock. At first glance he looked unpromising.

"Wow, he's a mess," said Stevie, echoing Carole's own thoughts. Although Lisa had managed to get most of the mud and grime off him, his body still showed the ravages of the wild. Carole noticed some distinct scratches.

"Looks like some sort of cat attacked him—maybe a bobcat?"

"I think Lisa mentioned that," said Stevie. "And it looks like the wound's getting infected, too," she said, pointing to the swelling as they approached the horse.

PJ stepped back as they came near him. They paused, willing to give him all the time he needed to get used to them.

"I'm sure he's a great horse and all," said Stevie. "But it's hard to imagine being obsessed with him." She now saw past the scratches, all the way to the visible ribs.

"Poor boy," said Carole. "He's had a rough time. I'm glad Lisa's been here for him."

"Yeah," Stevie agreed. "Just like I'm glad we're here for her. I think she needs our help as much as he needs hers."

"Definitely a Saddle Club project," Carole confirmed. "Now, if only we knew why she's acting so weird."

"Hi, guys. I wasn't sure if you'd be here yet," Lisa called from across the paddock. The two girls turned around and waved to their friend. "And I see you've met PJ. Isn't he great?"

"He seems a little nervous about us," Stevie said.

"That's just because I haven't introduced you properly yet. In a few minutes he'll be your best friend, too. He always behaves when he's being groomed or getting snacks. See you in a minute."

In a flash, Lisa had dropped off her school bag and was coming out of the main building, carrying a bucket and some sponges.

"I think it's time for a bath," she said. "And I think he's going to like it."

As she approached PJ, his ears perked up and his eyes seemed to brighten. It was as if Lisa had some kind of magic potion in the bucket. All the bucket held, though, was warm water and a little bit of shampoo.

Lisa clipped a couple of lead ropes to PJ's halter and walked him over to the shed, where she cross-tied him. He clearly trusted her as much as he had not trusted her friends. He regarded Carole and Stevie suspiciously all the way across the paddock. However, when they each picked up a moist sponge, his opinion of them seemed to improve. As soon as the three girls started washing him, he began behaving like a gentleman.

"Oh, this was the secret all along!" Lisa said, glad to see PJ so happy.

"Most horses seem to enjoy some aspect of grooming more than any other. I guess we know now that PJ's a bath guy!" Carole said, gently working the shampoo into his coat.

When they were finished with the shampoo, they rinsed him with clean water and then helped Lisa put the antibiotic ointment that Judy had left for him on all his wounds. Stevie and Carole were concerned about the meanlooking bobcat scratches. Lisa assured them that they were already getting better after two ointment treatments. Stevie was glad she hadn't seen the wound when it was more infected than it was now.

When PJ's coat was as shiny as it was going to get, Lisa gave him some more sandwich for a treat and promised she'd be back soon.

"I have to go ride a horse," she told her patient. "And when you get better, you can count on me riding you!"

Stevie and Carole exchanged glances. "Unless an owner claims him first," said Stevie.

"Nobody's called yet," said Lisa. "And CARL has advertised and called several vets. Maybe his owner didn't want him and never will claim him. I mean, what kind of sane person would let something like this happen to their horse?"

It wasn't a bad question. The girls took the bathing and grooming equipment back into the main building and picked up their book bags.

"Any response to the ads?" Lisa asked Anita.

"Not a word," she said. "And these just came from the printer. Want to post some?" She held up a thick batch of small posters showing a photograph of PJ with information about his rescue. Anyone who knew anything about him was urged to call CARL.

Stevie wasn't surprised to see Lisa almost recoil from the stack of posters. She'd clearly fallen in love with this wounded horse, and the idea that anybody else had ever owned him or ever would was painful to her. Stevie was afraid that her friend was in for a big disappointment. Under all the dirt and scratches was a good and probably valuable horse. It was clear that something had happened and the horse had gotten separated from its owner. Maybe PJ's owner hadn't seen the ad yet; maybe he hadn't heard from his vet yet. But he would. Stevie felt sure that this horse would be claimed, and Lisa would be hurt. She

63

hoped she and Carole would be able to help her see that PJ belonged with his owner, but that was going to be hard.

Finally Lisa took a couple of posters and the girls headed over to Pine Hollow.

"PJ's sick now, but he's getting better, and when he's all healed, if his owner hasn't shown up yet, he's going to need a place to stay," Carole said.

"Do you think?" Lisa asked, reading her mind.

"Well, I don't know. What do you think, Stevie?"

"It won't be easy," Stevie said.

They were all wondering the same thing: Would Max let PJ stay at Pine Hollow? That would make it easier for the girls to look after him. Although Max often worked with CARL, trying to help out when he had extra space in the stable for a temporary visitor, he usually asked for something in return, and that something was more work around the stable.

"He's going to expect us to clean every piece of tack in the tack room," Stevie said.

"And all the stuff he's got stored in the loft," Carole added.

"And the manure pile," Lisa said. "He's going to want it moved."

"Ugh," said Stevie.

"But it's for PJ!" Lisa reminded her.

"Yes, but it's *our* backs and hands," Carole said.

"To say nothing of our weekends," Stevie added.

"We'll still be at Pine Hollow," said Carole, looking on the bright side.

"And PJ would be there," said Lisa.

"All right," Carole consented.

"Count me in," said Stevie, suspecting that this would be more for Lisa than for PJ, but nonetheless willing.

Lisa was grinning by the time they arrived at Pine Hollow. She confidently led her friends into Max's office.

"To what do I owe this pleasure?" Max asked, glancing up from a pile of papers. He was looking wary already.

"Why, Max!" Stevie said. "Don't you trust us?"

"Not with *that* look on your faces. The last time the three of you came in here looking like that, I ended up hosting a herd of goats for a week."

"Nice goats," Stevie reminded him.

Max stifled a snort. "If you say so, Stevie. Okay, so what's up now?"

Lisa told him about PJ.

"Oh, right, the stray that Judy mentioned. Tangled with a bobcat, I guess. I hope his owner shows up soon," Max said. "They can't keep a horse at CARL for very long."

"Well, that's just the thing," Stevie said. "He's going to need a place to stay."

"Yes, he is," Max agreed.

The girls didn't say anything. They just looked at Max. He returned their stare.

Finally he sighed. "This is the sort of favor I can only do for my most responsible students," he said.

Stevie sighed, too. She knew they were about to enter the critical stage of negotiation.

"What's it going to be then?" she asked. "Tack cleaning? The manure pile?"

"Definitely tack," he said. "And I'd forgotten that the manure pile needs some attention, so I guess that, too."

Stevie felt Carole's glare and realized she'd blown it.

"What else?" she asked finally, breaking the silence.

"Well, we're going to have some visitors," he said.

"Horses?" Carole asked excitedly.

"And riders," said Max.

"Who?" Lisa asked.

"The Wainwright Jump Team."

"Really?" Carole asked.

"Here?" said Stevie.

"Who?" asked Lisa.

"They're this great jumping team," Carole said. "They

work together at a lot of the team jumping events. They always win tons of medals. I've read all about them in *Bits and Bridles*. They're really famous."

"And they don't like to have their horses stay on the grounds of the events where they're competing," Max said. "They go to local stables, feeling that it keeps the horses calmer. They rely on the stables to look after their horses properly."

"You mean *us*?" Stevie asked, getting the drift of Max's conversation.

"Not exactly," said Max. "They're very fussy and particular."

"And you're not?" said Stevie.

"No, I mean they're *much* fussier and more particular than I am. In fact, I wish they weren't coming, but I'm doing this as a favor to Dorothy DeSoto, who trained them." Dorothy was a former student of Max's and a former championship rider herself. When a spinal injury made her give up riding for good, she turned to training horses and coaching riders at her stable on Long Island.

"What I figure is that this foursome is going to turn the place upside down for three days the weekend after next, and I'm going to need all the help I can get doing everything I can for them. If you girls promise to make yourselves useful, I'll take this horse in—at least temporarily. Deal?"

The girls looked at one another. For them, helping out at Pine Hollow was as natural as breathing.

"Deal!" said Stevie, who was echoed by her friends.

That had been much easier than she'd thought. And she was sure they'd be far too busy with other things for Max to expect them to get to the manure pile!

After an hour of hard work in the stable, Stevie and Carole were ready to go on a trail ride.

"Race you to the creek," Stevie challenged Lisa.

"I don't think so," Lisa replied, picking up another bridle and beginning to apply saddle soap to it.

"It's been almost a week since you rode," Carole reminded her.

"I know, but we can't risk leaving some job undone. Max will never take PJ in if he doesn't think we're responsible."

Carole put her hands on her hips. "Max already thinks we're responsible," she said. "This is just his form of blackmail. We've been working hard. He'd think we were as deserving of a treat as we think we are."

"I don't know." Lisa wavered.

"Look, when this jumping team actually gets here, we can work ourselves crazy. For now, we need a little bit of fun," Stevie said.

68

Reluctantly Lisa put down the tack, stowed her cleaning gear, and picked up Prancer's very clean tack. "Okay," she relented.

As she walked out of the tack room ahead of her friends, Stevie and Carole shared a secret high five.

IT WAS BEGINNING to get dark when Lisa reached her doorstep. Normally she would have walked home with Stevie, but Stevie had said she needed to be home by six, and Lisa thought she could get in another forty-five minutes of tack cleaning before she had to leave for home. She glanced at her watch. It was nearly seven. She patted her back pocket. She could feel the sheets of paper she'd used to make the list of all the things she wanted to be sure to tell her parents. They'd all been so busy lately, she hadn't even had a chance to tell them much about PJ. Her mother could be wondering how the peanut butter was disappearing so fast from the jar! Lisa was sure it would make her mother laugh when she found out the answer to that. And

70

her father, who had always taught Lisa that hard work was as important as compassion, would be pleased with everything she'd been doing for PJ. Her hard work wasn't just helping the horse. It was helping CARL and Pine Hollow. And the compassion she felt—well, it was very real. That peanut butter–colored, peanut butter–loving horse had simply stolen her heart. She knew her parents would want to hear all about that.

She shifted the weight of her heavy backpack onto her other shoulder and opened the kitchen door. The lights were on, and her mother was sitting at the kitchen table.

"Finally!" her mother said.

It wasn't the welcome Lisa had expected. "Am I late?" she asked. Although it was seven o'clock, she often stayed at the stable that late. Surely her mother had known where she was.

"Well, you left the house before we were up this morning!"

"I left you a note," Lisa said.

"That's not good enough," said Mrs. Atwood. "Your father and I wanted to talk to you."

"And I wanted to talk with you, too," Lisa said defensively. "There's been a lot going on that I know you're going to want to hear about." She slid her backpack off her shoulder and lowered it to the kitchen floor. She reached for the papers in her pocket. "There's so much that I even made notes so I wouldn't forget. I wanted to talk to you last night, but you guys weren't home then, either."

"That's not the point," her mother said, slamming a plate down on the kitchen table.

Lisa didn't think her mother was being very logical, but she had the good sense not to push her point. Her mother was really crabby. Lisa slid papers back into her pocket. "I'll go change," she said.

She showered quickly and slipped into a pair of sweatpants and a T-shirt. She didn't want to keep her parents waiting any longer than necessary, especially if her mother was in such a foul mood. As a final thought, she stuffed her notes into the small pocket on the back of her sweats.

When Lisa got downstairs, she was surprised to see that there were just two plates set at the kitchen table, that her mother had forgotten place mats, and that the silverware had just been tossed by each plate. There were no napkins. Her mother was at the sink, staring out the window at something Lisa couldn't see.

Lisa straightened out the table setting quickly and efficiently and went over to the stove, where two hamburgers seemed to be overcooking. She put one on each plate, then added a spoonful of peas and some rice. She took the plates to the table, poured milk, and sat down.

Her mother hadn't moved since she'd returned to the kitchen. Lisa couldn't imagine what she'd done to make her mother so angry. Whatever it was, she knew her mother would get over it, but not until Lisa apologized.

"I'm sorry, Mom," she said.

Her mother didn't answer. She just hung her head.

Lisa stood up. "Mom?" She walked over to her mother. "I didn't mean to upset you," she said. "It's just that—"

"It's not you," Mrs. Atwood said softly.

"What is it?" Lisa asked, realizing that her mother was crying, hard. "What's going on?"

Her mother spoke without turning around. "Your father is leaving us," she said.

"He said something about a trip to California this month. Is that it?" Lisa asked. It always annoyed her mother when Mr. Atwood traveled on business.

"No, I mean he's leaving us," her mother said. "You. Me. For good." She turned back to the sink. Her face was streaked with tears, and her features were set in a grimace.

Lisa's father entered the kitchen. "We were hoping to talk with you this morning," he said.

"I left early," Lisa said matter-of-factly.

"I know," he said.

Lisa looked at him. He was holding his briefcase, almost

clutching it. It made Lisa think of the way she used to hold her teddy bear.

"We love you, you know that, don't you, Lisa?" he asked.

Of course she knew that. Everybody knew that. Parents loved their children.

"We've been having a hard time lately, Lisa. You must have noticed."

Everybody's parents argued. She remembered all the noise and arguing that went on at the Lake household.

"We may be able to work things out, but for now, your mother and I have to separate. It's the only way for us now. We love you. We both love you. Eleanor?"

"Yes, sweetheart, we love you very much," she parroted as if she'd been given a cue.

The kitchen timer dinged. Lisa sat down, staring at the hamburger in front of her as if it were a foreign object.

"I'm leaving now," said her father. He leaned over and gave Lisa a kiss on the top of her head. "I'll call you." It was just what he always said when he was going on a business trip. That must be it. An evening flight this time.

Lisa didn't move for a long time, and when she looked up, she was surprised to see her mother sitting at the table next to her. On the other side of the kitchen wall, they heard the familiar click, hum, and clank of the automatic garage door opening. There was a pause and then the sound began again, ending with a closing thud.

Lisa began picking at the hamburger and peas with her fork. She wasn't very hungry, but if she didn't eat, her mother would probably get really annoyed with her. She ate as much as she could, only vaguely aware that her mother didn't have any more appetite than she did.

Math problems, French vocabulary, and I need to read ahead in that book we're reading for English. Lisa made a mental to-do list. If she could get one or two chapters ahead, she'd be much better prepared for class the next day.

As soon as she'd finished eating, she stood up and cleared the table, leaving her mother with half a glass of wine to finish.

"Do you mind if I go do my homework?" Lisa asked. There wasn't much cleaning to be done anyway.

"Go ahead," said her mother. Dutifully, Lisa gave her mother a kiss, then went upstairs to her room.

She took the books she needed from her backpack and settled onto her bed. She started with *Great Expectations*. It was hard to concentrate, though. Something kept buzzing in her mind, something that wasn't right, something that didn't fit, something that needed to be fixed. She'd forgotten something, she knew. She'd made a mistake; she'd done something wrong.

She scratched her head and shifted from one side to the other.

"Ouch!" she said, feeling an uncomfortable lump under her bottom.

She moved back to her left hip and felt her backside with her right hand. There was a lump in the pocket of her sweats. She reached in and retrieved it. It wasn't really a lump. It was a sheaf of papers, crumpled and folded.

It took Lisa a few seconds to focus on what she held in her hand, and until she recognized it, she merely stared.

"Oh!" she said, startling the dog, who was lying at her feet. "I have to tell Mom and Dad about this stuff."

Then she really remembered. Her father was gone. He didn't care. He didn't want to know. He'd left them.

Lisa tossed the papers across the room and returned to *Great Expectations* with grim concentration.

8

LISA AWOKE WITH a start very early the next morning. Something was wrong. Something was different. It seemed vague and felt uncomfortable. She swallowed hard. *PJ*, she thought. *I have to get to PJ*. She sat up and then got out of bed.

The light that came through her window was the gray of dawn, still too early for her to need to be up, but not too early for PJ to need her. If she left now, she could spend more time with him, check those wounds, put ointment on them. She and the horse could even have a little talk before anyone else got there, and then she could go to school.

She was pretty sure the ointment was working. She

thought the swelling was going down. But cat scratches were dangerous, particularly from a wildcat whose claws could have awful germs on them from other things it had scratched or animals it had attacked.

Lisa got a chill just thinking about the infections that could be plaguing her horse. That beautiful light chestnut coat would become permanently scarred if she didn't take really good care of him. Judy had seemed confident that PJ would get better, but what if she was wrong?

And the swelling on PJ's ankle: Was it getting better? Lisa realized she'd been paying so much attention to the scratches that she had almost forgotten about the ankle. If the ankle didn't get better, nobody would ever be able to ride PJ.

"That horse was born for riding," Lisa whispered into her mirror. "I just know it."

She didn't even have to close her eyes to let her imagination soar. She could practically feel the powerful animal flying across an open field, loving every minute of freedom and union with a rider. And not just any rider. It would be Lisa.

Her parents had often considered getting her a horse. PJ's arrival at CARL was like a dream come true. It was fate: PJ was for her. They'd grow together and learn together. She knew that PJ's faith in her was boundless, and her confidence in him was infinite. They were a pair, inseparable.

All she had to do was . . . everything.

She dried her face, ran a comb though her hair, and hurried out of the bathroom. Two minutes to get her clothes on, another two in the kitchen, plus a scribbled note for her parents—no, just her mother, she reminded herself—and she was out the door with her backpack on her shoulder.

Lisa dropped her backpack by the paddock shed and then whistled for PJ. As soon as he spotted her, he trotted over. Lisa compared him to the reluctant and petulant horse she'd taken off Angus Rutherford's trailer just a few days before. He was still too thin, he was still scratched and scabbed, but he seemed to have gotten his heart and his spirit back—at least around Lisa. Besides, Lisa was sure that her special feeding program was helping to put some meat on his bones.

When he reached her, she gave him a hug. It was a careful hug because he still had plenty of wounds, and it made Lisa's heart soar to know that he trusted her enough to let her give him this affection. He tolerated her attention as he continued to sniff the air around her backpack.

"It's like we were meant to be together, don't you think, PJ?" she asked.

He snorted.

Lisa gave him his morning treat, and then she checked his sores.

Most of his cuts and abrasions were healing. There were even some signs that the hair was beginning to grow in again around most of them, though she knew he'd have some bare spots forever. When she got to the bobcat scratches, she wasn't as happy. The swelling was still there, maybe even a little greater, and the flesh around the scratches felt warm, which worried her. What if the infection had been spreading instead of healing? In her mind's eye, she could see the infection reaching other parts of PJ's body.

She sighed deeply, trying to get a grip on her emotions. She couldn't panic. That wouldn't help her at all, to say nothing of PJ. She could give him some more of the medicine. She found the tube of ointment in the shed and took a few minutes to spread the gooey stuff on the swollen scratches. As she did, she remembered the work she and her friends had done the day before, washing PJ's coat. What if they'd let in germs with the soap and water? Was it possible she was just making PJ sicker?

Don't panic, she reminded herself. *And don't be late to school.* She couldn't afford another half hour of detention.

"I'll be back this afternoon," she told the horse. He watched as she picked up her backpack and left the paddock, walking backward the whole way so that she could keep her eyes on him.

"See you—and while I'm gone, you get better, okay?"

PJ just bent his head and munched some grass in response.

CAROLE SMILED AS soon as she saw Stevie coming out of the school building. It was a nuisance that the three friends didn't all go to the same school, especially when two of them were trying to help the third. She was determined that they go to CARL together to be sure that Lisa spent some time at Pine Hollow that afternoon.

Stevie waved, clearly as glad to see Carole as Carole was to see her.

"We've got to go see Lisa again, don't we?" Stevie asked.

"Two great minds with a single thought," Carole agreed.

"You know, I'm glad Max wants us to work ourselves crazy. At least that'll help Lisa focus on something other than PJ. She sometimes goes a little off the deep end, doesn't she?"

Carole laughed. She was tempted to say something about pots and kettles calling one another black. Instead she settled for simple agreement. "Sometimes she does," she said. "And this is one of those times. I'm kind of worried about her in general, though."

"Me too," said Stevie. "She's been acting so different."

"And that's why we're here," Carole said.

"Besides, it means we get to help a horse in need while we're helping a friend in need."

"Perfect combination," said Carole.

"Look, there she is," said Stevie, pointing to Lisa, who stood in the paddock with PJ and Judy Barker.

"I hope everything's okay," said Carole. "With both of them."

"Let's go find out," Stevie said. They hurried over and joined their friend and the vet.

"Yes, I'm sure he's going to be fine," Judy was saying.

"But the swelling and the fact that it's warm around there—" Lisa protested.

"You're smart to notice these things, but it's part of the healing process. It means the horse's immune system is sending its reinforcements to the infected site. Just keep putting the antibiotic ointment on a couple times a day, and this boy will be fine very soon and ready to put on some more weight." Judy greeted Stevie and Carole, but their arrival didn't distract Lisa.

"And what about his leg?" Lisa asked. "Did you check that?"

"Yes, I did check it," said Judy. "The swelling has definitely gone down. He's not going to be ready to be ridden for a couple of weeks, but he's on the mend."

"How do you know?" Lisa asked.

"Well, I compared the swelling with the last time I saw him. Look, I'll show you." She took out her notes and showed Lisa that she'd measured the swelling carefully each time she'd seen the horse.

"The good news is that this horse is going to be ready to leave CARL by early next week. With any luck, we'll have found his owner by then."

Lisa flinched, and Carole knew why. Anybody who'd seen her with PJ over the last few days knew how attached she'd gotten to him.

Judy, who was often as wise about people as she was about horses, put her arm around Lisa's shoulder.

"Home is the best place for him," she said.

"We've convinced Max to take him in," said Lisa.

"And I bet you're going to have to work hard for him to make good on that promise!" Judy teased.

"It's worth it," Lisa said happily.

"He seems like a good horse," said Judy.

"The best," Lisa said.

"You've been working very hard with him," Judy praised.

"She sure has," Stevie confirmed. "She's here every morning and afternoon."

"Good nursing care is an important part of healing," Judy said. "Nice work, Lisa. And is everything okay?"

"As long as PJ is getting better," Lisa said.

"PJ is definitely getting better," Judy said. "What about you?"

"Me? Oh, I'm fine," Lisa assured her. "Just fine."

"Well, what this horse needs right now is a little rest. I've been watching him eye the shady corner of the paddock under the tree. So let's let him have a nap, okay?" Judy said.

"Just what we had in mind," Carole said. "We think there's just a tiny bit of work to be done at Pine Hollow."

"Oh, the old tack-cleaning ploy, eh?" Judy asked, smiling.

"That, and the manure pile," Stevie said.

"Oh dear!" Judy laughed.

"It's all worth it!" Lisa interjected. "Everything is worth it if we can save PJ!"

"Yes, of course," Judy said. "Well, I'll check in on him again in a couple of days. I'll see you then."

The girls said good-bye to Judy and PJ, then walked over to Pine Hollow together. Stevie and Carole were chatting about a project Stevie had to do for her math class. Carole recommended using beans because she could glue them to oak tag. Stevie had been thinking about macaroni because she could put it on strings.

"You can use all sorts of different colors of beans," Carole said. "And didn't you use beans once?" she turned to Lisa.

"I don't remember," Lisa said.

It was very unlike Lisa to forget anything she'd done for school.

"Come on, let's hurry," Lisa said. They were nearing the stable. She picked up her pace and then began to jog.

Even Carole never hurried when it came to mucking out stalls. She shrugged. "I guess she really loves this horse, huh?"

"Really," Stevie said.

The two of them followed Lisa into the stable. They put their backpacks and jackets in their cubbies, and by the time they walked down the aisle, Lisa was already halfway through cleaning Barq's stall. Carole and Stevie pitched in, bringing fresh shavings, water, and hay.

The rest of the afternoon went pretty much the same way: Lisa hurrying, Stevie and Carole trying to keep up. Lisa was a good worker. They were all good workers, and Max had told them that from time to time (though not often enough, in their opinions), but Stevie and Carole had never seen anything like the frenzy Lisa created that afternoon, cleaning everything in sight.

"Carole, look, there are cobwebs in Starlight's stall!" she said.

There were always cobwebs in stalls, Carole thought. Mostly she just ignored them. If there was a spider lurking there, it was probably eating flies and mosquitoes that would otherwise bite the horses.

"You'd better brush those out or Max might not let PJ stay here."

Carole didn't think a cobweb or two would interfere with Max's promise, but Lisa seemed to be in no mood for an argument. Obediently, Carole swiped at the cobwebs.

"And Stevie! Did you see how dirty the window in Belle's stall has gotten?"

The window in Belle's stall had always been clouded with dirt. Stevie didn't think there was enough window cleaner in the world to clean it. Lisa insisted that she try. Lisa had already cleaned the windows in Comanche's and Patch's stalls. Stevie went to take a look. They were actually clean!

When the last speck of dirt had been removed and the whole stable was practically clean enough for surgery, the three girls went into the locker area. Carole and Stevie thought they'd have a chance to drink a soda and take a little rest.

Lisa had a different idea. She appeared in the locker area and handed each of her friends a bridle, a sponge, and a can of saddle soap.

"What's gotten into you?" Stevie asked. "With all the cleaning we've done, Max would let us bring a whole herd of strays into this place!"

Lisa smiled. "I just want to be sure," she said. "I need to be sure." She picked up her sponge and got to work.

Even horse-craziest Carole knew that Lisa's zeal was totally out of proportion to the problem of getting PJ to be able to stay at Pine Hollow for a while. Something was going on, something else, and she thought she and Stevie deserved to know what it was.

"What's up, Lisa?" she asked.

"Nothing," Lisa insisted.

"Well, what's going on, then?" Stevie asked, joining in.

"Nothing's going on," Lisa said, shrugging.

"Well, you seem upset and out of—I don't know. Out of whack, I guess," Carole said. "Is everything okay?"

"Everything's okay," Lisa said. "The only thing that's going on is PJ. Oh, right, well, there is something else." She paused and stared at the bridle for a few seconds.

"Yes?" said Carole.

"My parents are getting a divorce. Dad left last night and I didn't have a chance to tell him all the things I've been doing with PJ."

Carole and Stevie's eyes widened and they stared at their friend in shock. Lisa didn't seem to register that anything was wrong, and she calmly resumed rubbing the bridle in her lap.

9

STEVIE OPENED HER mouth to speak, but she couldn't think of anything to say. She was overwhelmed with feelings, none of them expressible. *Divorce*. What a horrible word. What a horrible thought. Parents deciding they didn't love each other anymore. Leaving, breaking up, changing. What would it be like if it happened to her? But it wasn't happening to her, it was happening to Lisa, and it was almost unimaginable. And all the while, Lisa was just sitting there, rubbing a bridle until the old leather began to shine.

"There, I'm done with this bridle," said Lisa, standing up to put the tack in its place. "Nothing like cleaning tack to clear the mind, is there? Now, what comes next?" She sat back down on the bench. "I think we've done all the tack in here, but if I remember correctly, the driving tack is up in the loft. You know, I think PJ is not only going to be a fine school horse, but my guess—and my guesses about these kinds of things are usually right on target—is that he's going to be a fine driving horse, too. I mean, can't you just see that sweet boy pulling a cart or even a carriage of some kind? I wonder if Max is interested in getting into competitive driving more than he has been? Remember, we've tried it a couple of times and it's really very different from riding, though driving is still horses and that's what matters."

Driving? Carriages? What is Lisa talking about? Stevie asked herself.

"Well, I guess the first thing we're going to have to do is get PJ used to a saddle again. I mean, with all those scratches, it's probably been a while since he's been under saddle, and Judy says that his swollen leg is going to keep him out of the ring for another couple of weeks. Maybe there's still time to clean that driving tack. Maybe I should be getting home."

"Maybe," Carole said. "I bet your mother would like to have you with her at this time."

"I left the house early again," Lisa said. "I mean, I left a note and all, not that that kept my parents from freaking

90

out yesterday when I left a perfectly nice note. They said something about wanting to see me. Well, if they want to see me, they always know where to find me. It's either here or at CARL. I've got a lot of work to do. People count on me, you know. I guess I mean really that horses and other animals count on me, at least at CARL."

There was a pause in the flood of words and Stevie had the feeling there must be something to say, but she was still tongue-tied.

"So you're going home now?" Carole asked. It sounded more like a suggestion than a question.

"Okay," said Lisa. Without another word, she walked out of the room.

Stevie and Carole listened while their friend picked up her backpack and took her jacket out of her cubby. They heard her even steps retreating down the aisle.

"Divorce?" Stevie said, for the first time able to speak the word out loud.

"I guess," said Carole.

"Well, she seems to be taking it pretty well," Stevie said.

Carole regarded her quizzically.

"You mean she isn't?" Stevie asked.

"I don't think so," said Carole. "Look, we're her best friends in the whole world. She was with us for what, like, three hours before she finally told us. She announced it like she was telling us they were having chicken for dinner."

"And she didn't talk about it after that, did she?" Stevie said, understanding that that wasn't very much like Lisa. "I guess she's upset after all."

"Wouldn't you be?" Carole asked.

"That was the first thing I started thinking about," Stevie said. "I mean, how I would feel. I didn't like the thought at all. But I wasn't expecting this. I mean, her parents are always so quiet and reserved."

"You should have seen them the other morning," Carole said, and then she told Stevie about the incident with the milk.

"And?"

"It was so angry," said Carole.

"That doesn't sound unusual to me at all. My brothers talk to me like that all the time."

"Sure, and your parents probably gripe at one another sometimes, too. I know my parents did. Every family's different, though."

"You mean like we're weird that we yell at each other all the time?" Stevie asked.

"No. Not at all, that's normal—for you. Lisa and I have talked about it because we both live in such quiet homes. For us, it's just me and my dad and we sometimes get annoyed or angry with each other, like when I have to point out to him that he's not quite as perfect as he thinks he is." Carole smiled, thinking about her father.

"Well, he pretty much is," Stevie said.

"Anyway," Carole said, "we don't yell at each other, and that's normal for us. We do, however, on occasion, find it necessary to point out flaws in the other, like he has this silly notion that I spend too much time here. The point is that we say that stuff. In Lisa's house, Lisa's mother often criticizes her, but Lisa never returns it, and you never, ever hear her parents disagreeing about anything, even when it's clear that they don't agree. It's a little weird."

"Yeah," Stevie said, recalling examples of what Carole was talking about. She remembered a really awful dinner conversation about whether Mr. Atwood was going to cancel a business trip so that he could go to Mrs. Atwood's second cousin's niece's wedding. Even then, it hadn't made any sense, but nobody had raised their voices. In Stevie's family, nobody would have had such a dumb argument in the first place, but peas would fly across the table over lost homework.

"You know what it made me think?" Carole said. "It's like every family has its own volume level. Your family is definitely High. Whenever anybody has something to say, they say it or yell it or even throw it. And it's all on the surface. Dad and I talk to each other, too—we just do it without the flying food. The real trouble comes when nobody's talking. The Atwoods are set on Low, and until recently, like when Lisa began mentioning that her mother complained about all the traveling her father does, nobody ever snapped or complained to anybody about anything. When the volume changes, it means there's trouble."

"Like the milk thing?"

"Exactly," said Carole.

"And I guess what you're saying is that that milk thing wasn't any more about milk than Lisa's recent speech was about driving tack."

"Exactly," Carole said.

"Oh no," said Stevie.

"Exactly," Carole said again.

"And the only thing worse than a low volume going up is when it goes to Off," said Stevie.

"It's a good thing we're here to help her," said Carole.

"Exactly," said Stevie.

MRS. ATWOOD WAS standing at the sink when Lisa came in, almost exactly the same way she had stood the night before. This time, though, she was making a small salad.

"I'm home, Mom," Lisa said.

94

"Yes, I see, dear. Dinner will be ready in a few minutes. Why don't you clean up and then come give me a hand?"

"Okay," she agreed. She hurried upstairs to shower and change. It felt very normal. Her mother usually wanted her to help. Lisa usually had to shower and change first.

She noticed that the house seemed quiet. It wasn't because her father wasn't there. As her mother reminded her many times, he often wasn't there because he traveled so much. Lisa shrugged it off. She pulled on some clean and comfortable clothes and put her books on her desk so that she could do her homework as soon as she was finished with dinner.

Lisa always kept her room very tidy. Her mother insisted on it, but she would have done it anyway because it was her nature to be organized. It seemed a little odd, then, to see a crumpled mass of papers in the middle of her floor. She bent down to pick them up. She only had to begin to unfold them before she realized what it was. It was her list of all the good things she'd been doing—all the things she'd wanted to share with her parents, especially her father. She dropped the papers back on the floor and went downstairs.

Normal. That was how everything felt. Her mother was pulling a casserole out of the oven, and the table needed to be set.

Lisa pulled three place mats, three forks, and three knives out of the drawer. Then she realized her mistake and replaced one mat and one set of silverware, hoping her mother hadn't seen her error. One look and she knew that her mother had. She didn't say anything, though.

Lisa put the settings on the table, poured a glass of milk for herself, and asked her mother what she wanted.

"I'll have milk, too," said Mrs. Atwood.

That was odd. She usually had a glass of wine with dinner, even when it was just the two of them.

Lisa gave her mother milk. She brought the salad over to the table and put out plates for each of them. Her mother brought the casserole to the table, and they sat down. Mrs. Atwood served Lisa a plate and then served herself. Lisa gave herself some salad and then passed the bowl over to her mother.

They ate.

"Where's Dad?" Lisa broke the uncomfortable silence.

Her mother looked stunned. "We told you. We're separated," she answered.

"I know, but where is he?" she asked.

Mrs. Atwood appeared shaken. "He's staying in a hotel downtown for now," she said. Then her voice wavered. "Once the divorce is final, he's moving to California."

Lisa stood up and took her plate, stacked her mother's

on top of it, and walked toward the sink. The world around her seemed to melt a bit, distorted like one of those mirrors in a fun house.

"Mom—" she began.

"Don't worry," said Mrs. Atwood. "I'll do the dishes. You can just get to your homework."

Lisa felt the plates slip out of her hand. There must have been a sound, a loud one, but she didn't hear it.

"Okay," she said mechanically. Then she went up to her room and started her homework.

NOTHING MAX COULD have said would have prepared The Saddle Club for the Wainwright Jump Team.

"Let me see if I've got this right," Stevie said to Carole. "Mrs. Wainwright has Red measuring the temperature of her horse's drinking water?"

"You've got it right. I guess 'cold' isn't good enough. It's got to be exactly forty-three degrees Fahrenheit," Carole told her.

"Mr. Wainwright isn't so fussy, though. He told Denise it needed to be between forty-three and forty-five degrees. Max warned us, didn't he?"

" 'Fussy' really didn't cover this. How can Red stand it?"

"Easy," said Carole. "He can stand it because you and I are doing everything else."

"Where's Lisa?" Stevie asked, realizing that their threesome was looking a lot more like a twosome.

"She's with PJ," Carole said.

Judy had given PJ a clean bill of health on Thursday, and Lisa had brought him over to Pine Hollow Thursday afternoon. It was a short walk from CARL, so she hadn't even needed to wait until she could get someone to drive a van. She hadn't wanted to waste a second until she got him to Pine Hollow.

"I see what you mean," Max had said, admiring his newest tenant. He gave PJ a pat on his face. The horse flinched. "Did I hurt him?" he asked.

Lisa shook her head. "No," she said. "He's just like that sometimes with people he doesn't know."

"Well, I hope you'll arrange an introduction for me soon," he teased.

Lisa hadn't thought it was a funny joke. In fact, it worried her. If PJ misbehaved, Max might say he couldn't stay at Pine Hollow no matter how many chores she and her friends did. Lisa couldn't let that happen. The only way to make sure he didn't misbehave was if she was with him and kept him from misbehaving.

A day later PJ was still edgy, and Lisa was unwilling to leave his side.

"I guess we have to let her stay with him, huh?" Carole said, thinking about PJ's behavior.

"It seems to me we're making a lot of allowances for her, Carole," Stevie said.

"But her parents . . . ," Carole said.

"Right, and we know she's going nuts about this horse. But it turns out that we're doing all the work that's making Max agree to let PJ stay here."

"You! What's your name?" A voice boomed behind her. Stevie turned. It was Mr. Wainwright. She wasn't absolutely sure she wanted him to know her name, but she had to cooperate for Max's sake.

"Stevie Lake," she said.

"What kind of name is that?" he demanded.

"Short for Stephanie," she said, though she didn't think he had the right to insult her name. *His* name was Marion. Stevie kept her thoughts to herself.

"Where's the hoof polish?" he asked.

"In the cabinet in the tack room," Stevie told him. "Right over there." She pointed.

"Get it for me, please," he said.

Now she was in a quandary. The Saddle Club's job was to do everything but work for the Wainwrights. On the other hand, their job really was to make Max happy, and Stevie had the sneaking suspicion that keeping the Wainwrights happy would keep Max happy.

"Of course, sir," she said.

As soon as she delivered the pot of polish to Mr. Wainwright, she hurried back to Barq's stall, which she and Carole had been mucking out together.

"We'd better hurry," Carole said. "It's almost time for the afternoon feeding."

"And watering," said Stevie. "Do you think the stable horses are going to die of jealousy if they just get cold tap water, not cooled to forty-three degrees?"

"Don't tell them, okay? As long as they don't hear about it, we'll be safe." The girls laughed.

The entire stable was abuzz with activities centering around the adored and pampered horses of the jumping team. There were four riders on the team, but only Mr. and Mrs. Wainwright were at the stable that afternoon. Their competition was starting the next day, and the horses would be there for a good part of it. It was something everybody at the stable was looking forward to.

"O'Malley!" cried Mrs. Wainwright. "Where's the special grain blend?"

Nobody ever called Red "O'Malley." Stevie and Carole gaped while he rushed to bring her the "special grain blend." He didn't even make a face or a smart remark. He didn't even look as if he minded when she apparently forgot to say thank you.

"How do you suppose Dorothy stands it?" Carole asked. She really felt sorry for their friend, who worked on training these jumpers.

"I think she stands it by sending them to every competition in the country so that they're never anywhere near her stable," Stevie said.

"Clever woman," said Carole.

The girls finished the mucking and then handed out feed to each of the horses, plus fresh hay and water (from the tap, no ice). When they were done, they decided they'd earned a break and went to find Lisa.

She and PJ were in the schooling ring, far away from the hubbub inside the stable.

"Everything okay?" Stevie asked, climbing onto the fence.

"Just fine," said Lisa. "I thought he might like some fresh air. He probably got used to being outdoors while he was lost in the woods. I think it's a little, well, claustrophobic for him inside."

"You mean you couldn't stand one more second of those people?" Carole whispered. The last thing they needed was to get the Wainwrights angry at them.

102

"More or less," Lisa conceded.

She had PJ on a lead rope and was walking him slowly around the ring, letting him sniff and explore. "One of these days I'm going to be able to ride him here," she said. "I want him to be used to the place. That's a good idea, isn't it?" she asked Carole.

"Seems like a good idea to me," said Carole. "Most horses adjust to new surroundings fairly quickly, but there's nothing wrong with helping them along."

PJ flinched at a stack of cavalletti.

"He's seen these three times before," said Lisa.

"Well, maybe the next time around will go more smoothly," Carole suggested.

Carole and Stevie perched on the top rail of the fence and watched their friend lead PJ slowly around the far end of the ring.

"She hasn't said another word about her parents' divorce to me," Stevie said. "Has she talked about it with you?"

"No," Carole said. "All she ever talks about is PJ."

"I suppose that means her volume is still off?" Stevie asked.

"Yeah, and the receiver's on the blink, too," said Carole.

"What do you mean?" Stevie asked.

"Watch her with PJ," said Carole. "He's okay with her,

but he still misbehaves with almost everybody else. She's decided he's the world's most perfect horse. It's possible that he might become the world's most perfect horse, but right now he seems as tender and vulnerable as—well, I guess as vulnerable as Lisa."

"Think he'll change?"

"Only time will tell," said Carole. "He must have had a pretty awful experience out in the wild. Maybe that changed him once and it's just a matter of changing him back. Or maybe he's always been like that. I don't know, and neither does Lisa."

"So this is where you've come to get out of the line of fire!" The girls turned to see Mrs. Reg coming out of the stable toward them.

"Do you need us?" Carole asked. She hoped the answer was no.

"No," she said. "I'm just glad to have a little breather myself. I don't want to be there when Marion Wainwright figures out that the water is actually fifty-one degrees. I'd rather watch Lisa give that horse a walk."

Mrs. Reg leaned against the fence, relaxing, until Lisa joined them.

"I think he's more confident now," Lisa said. "Maybe that's enough walking for a while, anyway. His leg is still swollen, you know."

"I know," said Mrs. Reg. "Judy says it'll be healed in another couple of weeks. Maybe you'd better put him in his stall."

Lisa took the horse back inside. Carole and Stevie began to lower themselves from the fence and return to their chores, but Mrs. Reg began speaking.

"You know," Mrs. Reg said, "there was a pony once."

It was going to be one of Mrs. Reg's stories. There never seemed to be any warning when she launched into one, and there was no more a way of telling how long it was going to be than there was of telling what it was about. The woman just loved to tell stories about horses, and the riders at Pine Hollow were expected to sit still and listen. Carole and Stevie got comfortable on the fence.

"This old boy lived with a farmer who abused him. It wasn't that he was mean; he just couldn't take care of him. The owner was too old. Sometimes he'd sleep a whole day away without feeding the pony or giving him fresh water. Sometimes he'd forget. The animal rescue people spotted him, all bony and unbrushed, and took matters into their own hands. This was before the days of CARL, you know."

It was hard to imagine that there had been days before CARL. The place was always so busy that many, many animals must have suffered without its kind help.

"Well, before CARL, the animal owners and lovers in

the area would just all pitch in in their own ways. The lawmen decided it was time for us to pitch in. They called my Max"—that meant her husband, Max's father—"and they delivered the pony to us on a Saturday morning. No, I think it was a Friday. It was the same day the feed man used to come, and his regular delivery was always, uh, Tuesday. Yes, Tuesday."

It didn't matter to the girls what day it was, but it seemed important to Mrs. Reg to be specific. Stevie and Carole knew better than to interrupt. They remained silent.

"Tuesday. Definitely." She seemed pleased, and she continued. "He was unhappy from the minute he walked into the place."

"How could any horse—?" Stevie started. Mrs. Reg glared at her. Stevie stopped talking.

"He nipped at anyone who walked by, human or horse. If we put a saddle on him, he'd puff like nobody's business. Sometimes it took four tries to get the girth tight enough. He was so naughty with a rider on him that the youngsters began yanking on his mouth. Worst possible thing, of course. That made him even crankier. That made them yank more. Not that my Max would let them get away with that any more than Max does today. He wasn't young, you know."

"Your Max?" Carole asked.

106

"No, the pony," Mrs. Reg snapped. "I don't even remember his name now. Anyway, my Max figured he'd never be able to retrain him and make him into a good school pony, and he couldn't keep using him the way he behaved. He gave up on him."

"He sold him?" Carole asked.

"No. He gave the pony away. He hadn't paid anything for the creature; he certainly wasn't going to charge anyone else for him. He gave him to a woman who had a field where he could live out his days."

"Then what happened?" Carole asked. She had the feeling Mrs. Reg was about to walk away, as she often did, just when the story was getting interesting.

"He eventually got used to being treated well," said Mrs. Reg. "Oh, look! Mr. Wainwright is waving his arms about something. I've got to go rescue Red. And you girls should go give Barq a grooming. He needs it."

She left them scrambling down the fence.

"What was that about?" Stevie asked Carole. "Was that another weird Mrs. Reg story?"

"I don't think so," said Carole. "I think she's telling us that PJ is having trouble adjusting and he might not make it here," she said. "It's a good thing she didn't tell that to Lisa."

"Maybe," said Stevie.

THE AFTERNOON DIDN'T slow down after that. It only seemed to get busier. The Wainwrights kept waving their arms and people kept doing whatever they commanded.

When Carole stepped into the tack room to pick up a longe line for Mr. Wainwright, she found Red tucked into a dark corner.

"What are you doing here?" she asked.

"Hiding," he admitted readily. "Since that man refuses to do anything for himself, it's a sure bet he'll never come in here. I thought I'd get a moment's peace."

"Your secret's safe with me," Carole said, chuckling. "But remember, while you're hiding, he's ordering other people around. Here's the longe line he asked me for."

"Yeah, well the last time I took that one to him, he rejected it, saying it was too old."

"Then I'll tell him it's our *new* longe line and see how he likes that. Or maybe that it's the one we save for the best horses. What do you think?"

"Go with the best horses thing. And give me five more minutes, okay?"

"Okay," Carole said, taking the longe line with her as she left. She delivered it to Mrs. Wainwright with the "best horses" message. Mrs. Wainwright smiled. So did Carole, who quickly escaped down the stable aisle.

"Look at this, Carole!" Lisa called out to her. Carole paused. Once again, Lisa was grooming PJ. It seemed to be the one activity he would always tolerate—well, that and eating. There was no doubt about it. The horse was getting better. His ribs were no longer so prominent, and the constant brushing, combing, and rubbing of his coat was bringing out a distinct sheen.

"You've got that coat shinier than the Wainwrights' horses'," Carole said.

"I know," said Lisa. "Isn't it wonderful?"

Carole sighed and swallowed the words she wanted to say. Carole and Stevie were working like crazy at Pine Hollow just to help their friend, and the only thing Lisa could think to do was groom PJ one more time.

"It's wonderful," Carole agreed, reminding herself that Lisa was going through a very hard time. Normally Lisa would have been the first to recognize what was fair and what wasn't. The fact that she couldn't do that now was a measure of how much she needed support from her friends. Carole was willing to overlook her actions for a while.

"I've got to get to work," said Carole. "Mrs. Reg asked me to assign ponies for the lesson Max is giving after this class. If I don't do it right, Penny will have six lessons today and none tomorrow. All the little kids are crazy about her! See you!"

"Okay," Lisa said, picking up another brush.

Carole met Stevie in Mrs. Reg's office. Mrs. Reg was laying out the grooming tools for the Wainwrights' horses as if they were a surgeon's tools (and as if the Wainwrights couldn't do that for themselves). Carole sat in Mrs. Reg's chair with the daily horse chart spread out in front of her. Stevie sat across from her with the list of students for the next class. Through the window the girls could see Max giving a class for intermediate riders. Beginners were next.

"Okay," Stevie began. "Alice?"

"Let's put her on Dime," said Carole, penciling in the assignment.

110

"Then what about Taisha? She always wants to ride Dime."

"She should try another horse," said Carole. "How about Peso?"

"Peso behaves better with boys," Stevie reminded her. "So, if we put her on Nickel, then we can have Peter ride Peso."

"But Peter cantered last week on Dime. He's going to want to ride him again." She sighed and took out her eraser. "And the only other boy in that class is David, and he just grew a whole lot, so he's way too big for Peso, so maybe nobody should ride Peso this lesson."

Stevie looked over her shoulder at the chart. "But nobody's ridden Peso all day long," she said.

Carole started erasing and was still erasing when the phone rang. Since Mrs. Reg and Red were busy with the Wainwrights and Max was teaching a class, the only thing for Stevie to do was to answer it.

"Pine Hollow Stables," she said, trying to sound very professional.

"Hi, my name is Crawford, Louis Crawford."

"Yes, Mr. Crawford. What can we do for you?" she asked. It sounded like something Mrs. Reg might say. "Both the Regnerys are busy now, but I'll try to help you if I can."

"I lost my horse," he said. "I mean, my horse got loose when a drunk driver knocked down a couple of fence posts."

"Oh, how terrible," Stevie said. She could hardly imagine how she would feel if she'd lost her horse. "You can advertise in the local papers or put up flyers. I'm sure that would help. People around here are good about taking care of animals. Actually, there's a place called CARL—"

"Right, I know about that," said Mr. Crawford. "They put out some flyers recently and I got a call from my vet, too. I saw the photograph. I just know it's Protocol. When I called CARL, they told me he was staying at Pine Hollow."

"There's no horse here by that name," said Stevie. Even as she said it, she knew it was a dumb thing to say.

"I'm sure they gave me the right number. You did say this is Pine Hollow, right?"

"Right, Pine Hollow," Stevie echoed.

"Well, look, why don't you have the Regnerys call me when they have a minute and we'll see what the situation is."

"Right. I'll do that," said Stevie. She pulled the phone message pad over to her and borrowed Carole's pencil. She wrote down his name, phone number, and the words *lost horse*. Then she hung up the phone and handed the pencil back to Carole.

112

"PJ?" Carole asked.

Stevie nodded.

"Oh, no."

Stevie lowered herself back into the chair and stared at the message.

"I could lose it," she said.

"He'd call again. You didn't sound too swift there. I'm sure he'll call again."

"I'll put it at the bottom of the messages," Stevie suggested.

"Below the calls from people who want Mrs. Reg to change telephone companies?" Carole asked.

Stevie shrugged. "It might work."

"He'll still call again," Carole repeated. "And then Mrs. Reg would be annoyed with you."

"What would I be annoyed about?" Mrs. Reg asked, entering the office. "I mean, is it possible that there would be anything in the world more annoying than those people Dorothy DeSoto forced on us?" Carole started to stand up to relinquish her chair to Mrs. Reg, but Mrs. Reg shook her off and, instead, chose to stand in a corner, out of sight from the aisle.

Carole couldn't help laughing. "That's exactly the same thing Red was doing in the tack room," she said.

"He was my inspiration," said Mrs. Reg. "Five minutes, that's all I ask! Now, what's going on here?"

A little reluctantly, Stevie handed her the phone message.

"Lisa's horse?" Mrs. Reg asked. Stevie nodded.

"Sounds like it," Carole confirmed.

"Well, we'd better call this man," she said, reaching for the phone.

It didn't take long to confirm their worst suspicions. Mr. Crawford described PJ extremely accurately. There was no doubt. Mrs. Reg took some time describing PJ's wounds and all the care he'd gotten at CARL and at Pine Hollow.

"Right, right. Well, of course, we're in the horse business, but we also care," said Mrs. Reg. "He's gotten a lot of attention from some of our young riders." There was a pause. "Well, of course I saw that. He's been difficult as well. But we've looked after him. You can get full details from Judy Barker. Yes, that's our vet. Right. And we all think your horse tangled with a bobcat. He's got scars. And you should have seen the dirt!"

The two of them talked for a few more minutes, then Mrs. Reg hung up after a final "Okay, we'll see you soon."

She sighed and looked at Carole and Stevie.

"Protocol. That's the horse's name. He's definitely talking about the same horse. In the meantime, you might want to let Lisa know so that she can have him ready to go."

"When's the man coming?" Carole asked.

"Well, he lives in Cross County. I don't think it will be long. Maybe twenty minutes."

Carole handed the horse-and-rider charts to Mrs. Reg. "We've got work to do," she said.

"WHERE IS SHE?" Stevie asked, looking around the stable. "I mean, the last time we saw her, she was grooming PJ for what, the third time today?"

"In his stall," Carole said. "And he's not there. Neither is she."

"Maybe she's taken him for another walk," Stevie said. She and Carole left the stable and walked over to the schooling ring, where the Wainwrights were longeing one of their horses. There was no sign of Lisa or PJ.

"You don't suppose she heard the phone call and has run away or anything, do you?" Stevie asked.

"Stevie, that's the sort of thing you'd do, not Lisa," Carole said.

"Well, the old Lisa was pretty predictable that way. The new one, I don't know. I think the word is *obsessive*."

"I think the word is *she needs our help*," Carole reminded her. "Come on, let's find her."

It didn't take long. They spotted Lisa and PJ in the paddock across the drive from Pine Hollow. It was a

115

particularly nice area with a small hill that allowed a beautiful view of Pine Hollow and all the surrounding countryside.

"I think she must be trying to give him an overview of the place," Stevie said, joking.

"Maybe, but it doesn't seem to be working," Carole observed.

Stevie looked to see what she was talking about. PJ was acting up a bit. He wasn't misbehaving to a dangerous degree, but he was tugging at the lead rope and being generally uncooperative.

"She loves him anyway," said Stevie.

"Well, she clings to him, that's for sure. Obsessed, that was what you said, right?"

"I heard it on an afternoon talk show," Stevie said. "It's what I got for staying home with a cold one day."

Carole, afraid that Stevie was going to launch into a full-scale explanation of obsession as defined by a talk-show host, spoke up. "Let's go give her a hand. The only time that boy stands still and behaves completely is when he's being fed or groomed. Any other time he's more than a little frisky. I think Lisa needs our help." She walked up the hill toward her friend. As she climbed, she remembered the phone call and the news she and Stevie had to give to Lisa. She slowed down.

Behind her, Stevie was lagging as well.

"We don't have to tell her first thing," Stevie said.

Carole agreed.

They joined Lisa at the crest of the hill. As soon as all three of them began patting PJ, he responded by improving his behavior.

"He does like to be the center of attention," Stevie teased.

"Wouldn't you if you'd been through the ordeal he must have had in the wild?"

"I guess," Stevie said. "Though I suspect he's always been just a little bit pampered."

"And as long as I'm looking after him, he'll be pampered even *more*," Lisa said.

It was a cue. As soon as Carole heard her say that, she knew it was the moment to tell her. She took a breath. "Uh, Lisa—" she began.

"I wish someone would spoil me like that!" said Stevie.

The moment was gone. Carole let out her breath.

"Oh, Stevie!" Lisa teased. "You can groom yourself!" The three of them laughed together at the idea of Stevie being brushed and coddled by three people all at once.

"Come on, let's walk back to the stable," Carole suggested. "Max may need us to do something."

"You guys have been working hard, doing all those chores just for PJ," Lisa said. "I haven't been much use except to look after him. I can't wait until he's better and I can ride him. Max will see what a wonderful horse he is and he'll be glad he let him come to Pine Hollow!"

She looked up at the horse and put her arm around his neck, impulsively giving him a hug. He pulled back, almost snapping her arm off to free himself. She blew him a kiss instead.

"Some guys just don't like public displays of affection," she said.

"I guess you're right," Stevie said.

They walked together in silence, Carole and Stevie both wondering how—or even more importantly *if*—they were going to give the news to Lisa. They remained silent as they walked back across the driveway and took PJ into the jumping ring, which was empty now. Lisa unclipped his lead rope. PJ shook his head as if to shake out his mane, and then trotted to the far side, away from The Saddle Club.

"Lisa—" Carole began.

"What's that?" Lisa interrupted, watching a horse van pull into the driveway. "You don't suppose those Wainwrights are bringing some other horses over here to bother us even more."

"I don't think so," said Stevie. "Lisa, I think that's—"

"Who's he?" Lisa asked, looking at the man who got out of the cab of the van.

"I think his name's Crawford," said Stevie.

The man looked around, but it didn't take him long to find what he was looking for. He strode over to where the girls stood at the edge of the ring.

"Pro!" he called out. The girls looked at the object of his call. Across the ring, PJ's ears perked up immediately. He snorted, flicked his tail, and trotted over to where they stood.

Lisa looked a little confused, but she reached out her arms to welcome the horse. PJ never even looked at her. He headed straight for Mr. Crawford, who put his arms around the horse's neck. PJ didn't object one tiny bit. Mr. Crawford grinned.

"Who are you?" Lisa demanded.

"My name's Louis Crawford," he said. "I called a little while ago. Was it you I spoke with?"

"Me," Stevie said. "I'm Stevie. This is Lisa, and Carole."

"What's going on?" Lisa asked.

"Mr. Crawford is PJ's owner," Stevie said.

"No, he's mine!" Lisa said.

"Well, he's certainly thrived in your care," said Mr. Crawford. "When I spoke with Dr. Barker, she told me what bad condition he was in when he arrived. She told me there was a girl who was looking after him. Liza?"

"Lisa," the girls corrected him.

"Lisa, I guess Pro and I owe you a debt of gratitude."

"Pro?" Lisa asked.

"Protocol," he said. "That's his name. What is it you've been calling him?"

"PJ," said Lisa. "Because—"

"He's the color of peanut butter, right?"

Carole looked at Lisa to see how she would answer that. But it didn't seem that she could, or would. She looked totally exhausted, as if the simple explanation of giving the horse her sandwich was more than she could manage.

"Yeah," she said finally.

Max and Mrs. Reg walked up to them. Max introduced himself and his mother.

"Oh, yes, we spoke," said Mr. Crawford.

Carole and Stevie stood back to let the adults talk. Lisa hadn't moved. Carole didn't think she could.

Their conversation was warm and cordial. Mr. Crawford kept saying how wonderful it was to see his horse, how much he loved the animal, how grateful he was for all the veterinary care he'd gotten, and how wonderful it was that "these girls" had done such a good job looking after him since he'd arrived here.

"I'll gladly pay you board for the time he's been here," Mr. Crawford said.

"Oh, it's only been a couple of days," said Max. "It's nothing. If you'd like, you could make a donation to CARL and see to his vet bills."

"Anything, anything," said Mr. Crawford.

Carole listened to the words, but she watched the horse and she watched her friend. The horse stood absolutely quiet right next to Mr. Crawford during the entire conversation. There was no fussing, no flinching, no misbehavior of any kind, even when Mrs. Wainwright brought one of her feisty horses out of the stable into the jumping ring, walking it right behind Pro. When Mr. Crawford reached up to pat his horse, the horse didn't pull back or nip as he often did with others who weren't feeding or grooming him.

Lisa, like Carole, was not watching the adults. In fact, Carole suspected that Lisa wasn't even hearing their conversation, never heard all the nice things and the thanks Mr. Crawford expressed to her about looking after his horse. Lisa never took her eyes off PJ.

When the conversation ended, Mr. Crawford snapped

his fingers and Pro followed him, without a lead rope, through the gate and over to the van.

"This guy is sometimes pretty naughty around other people," said Mr. Crawford.

"We'd noticed that," Max joked. "And there are a couple of horses here who won't miss him at all!"

The men and Mrs. Reg laughed. Carole and Stevie stood by, prepared to help Mr. Crawford load PJ into the van, but he didn't need any help. PJ simply walked up the ramp and obediently waited to be cross-tied for security.

Mr. Crawford slammed the door shut and then shook the Regnerys' hands. He thanked Carole and Stevie and waved to Lisa, who was still standing in the ring. Then he pulled out of the driveway and was gone.

Max, Mrs. Reg, Carole, and Stevie all turned to look at Lisa. Her back was to them and her head was hanging. They walked over to her.

At first Carole couldn't hear anything. She became aware that Lisa was crying only because her shoulders were heaving up and down. The next thing she noticed was that drops of tears were falling onto Lisa's paddock boots.

Stevie got to her first and put her arms around her. Lisa didn't resist, didn't even seem to notice.

Carole reached her next. She joined in the hug.

"I'll get you girls a box of tissues," Mrs. Reg said very sensibly. Max delivered the tissues a few seconds later and directed the girls to the picnic table in the backyard of the house.

"You'll have some privacy there," he said. "You know where to find me."

Together, Stevie and Carole took Lisa over to the table.

It took a long time, Carole thought later, for Lisa to begin talking. At first all she could talk about was PJ, and both Carole and Stevie knew instinctively that saying anything sensible like "he wasn't yours" or "he behaved much better with his owner" wasn't going to do any good. This crying wasn't logical. In fact, Carole was pretty sure it wasn't even about PJ.

When Lisa finally wailed, "And I never got to show him to my dad!" the girls knew they were making progress.

"I wanted him to know what a wonderful job I was doing, but I didn't tell him about all the things I was up to and I made that whole list but he left anyway and if I hadn't left so early in the morning maybe he would have seen the list or I suppose I could have shown it to Mom, but it was Dad who needed to see it because I'm a good girl, a good daughter, and I try to do everything right, but he doesn't believe me because he's gone—just like PJ—*gone!*"

123

Stevie and Carole both hugged her.

And when she finally stopped crying, Stevie and Carole gathered her things and walked her home. It was time for her to talk with her mother.

Mrs. Atwood took one look at her daughter coming up the walkway with her two best friends and reached out. Lisa walked straight into her arms.

12

"I DON'T THINK I realized divorce meant so much crying," Stevie said to Carole the following Saturday. The two of them had gotten to Pine Hollow early—early enough to see Lisa get out of her mother's car with her face still blotched from crying. She had her bag of riding clothes, plus another bag. She looked more angry than sad and barely spoke with her friends before she stuffed her bags into her cubby and stomped back outside for their Pony Club meeting.

"I don't think I realized it, either," said Carole. "But I've got to say I think crying is probably healthier than clinging to a horse the way Lisa clung to PJ, or Pro, or whatever his name is. You know, though, I think I was a little bit like that when my mother was dying. Even when everything else in the world was going wrong, horses were still going right."

"It's not exactly the same," said Stevie. "You were just overattached to horses, exactly the way you are today!"

"Sort of," said Carole. "Anyway, let's go see if she remembered to save us seats."

Carole and Stevie found Lisa on the bench at the indoor ring. She'd saved one seat on either side of her for her friends. They slipped onto the benches and were glad for a moment to chat.

"What are you up to this afternoon?" Carole asked.

"Yeah, why can't you come over to my house?" Stevie asked.

"My dad is supposed to come pick me up here," Lisa said. Her jaw was set stiffly.

"That'll be neat," Stevie tried.

"Right. Well, he's coming because some judge told him he had to," Lisa explained. "I'm sure that's why he's doing it."

"What?" Carole asked.

"Custody stuff," Stevie said. "It's what lawyers argue about in divorces."

"They're only separated," Lisa reminded her friends.

Max called the meeting to order.

"Well, it's nice to have the place to ourselves!" he began. Everybody laughed because they had noticed what nuisances the Wainwrights had been the weekend before. "You'll all be pleased to know that the Wainwrights did very well in their show last weekend. So well, in fact, that they qualified to compete in another show this week, in Oregon!"

Everybody broke into applause. Carole laughed. A stranger watching might have assumed that they were pleased at the Wainwrights' success, but what they were really pleased about was the distance.

"And the week after, they'll be in Pennsylvania." The applause stopped. "Western Pennsylvania," he said. The cheering began again.

"Enough, enough. Now, some of you must have watched them longeing their horses and seen what wonderful exercise it was. What we're going to do today is work on longeing techniques. I think we all need a treat, so after our meeting we're going to make small teams—two, three, four, whatever you like—and go on a trail ride. The weather's nice, and I think it will be good for us all."

Even Lisa smiled, contemplating that.

The Pony Club meeting went very fast. It seemed like

only minutes until the riders were tacking up for a trail ride.

Lisa paused before entering the tack room. She'd dreamed so fiercely about riding PJ that it felt odd to be picking up Prancer's tack. The dream had been almost real. She sighed, swallowing the lump in her throat and holding back her tears.

Prancer's saddle and bridle felt strangely comfortable in her hands as she carried them to her stall. Prancer stood politely while she tacked her up, and she didn't puff out at all.

"You're being cooperative today," she said. Then she remembered: Prancer was almost always cooperative. She patted her, and the mare flicked her ears affectionately.

Of course The Saddle Club had decided to ride together, and there was no question about what their destination would be. They'd ride to Willow Creek. They checked their watches and confirmed with Max what time he expected them back, and then they were off.

It all felt so normal to Lisa. There she was with her friends, the best friends anyone could ever have, doing the thing they loved the most. It was almost possible to forget, for a moment at a time, anyway, that everything was wrong. Her father was gone and PJ was gone.

"Race you to the creek!" Carole said.

128

Automatically, Lisa nudged Prancer to a canter, leaving her thoughts in the woods behind her. Stevie won.

When they'd finished dipping their feet in the rushing creek, finished watering their horses, and finished talking about longeing, they returned to Pine Hollow. Lisa's heart became heavier and heavier as she saw the stable come into view and recognized her father's car in the parking area.

"I'm not going with him, you know," she said to her friends.

"Lisa!" said Carole.

"Why not?" Stevie asked.

"I don't want to. I'll see him. He's here. But I'm not going anywhere with him."

Carole and Stevie didn't argue with her.

When they arrived at the stable, Lisa returned her father's wave and indicated that she had some work to do. Then, in a very businesslike manner, she went about doing it.

Carole didn't think Lisa had ever given Prancer a better grooming, and she didn't think it was because of any special techniques Lisa had picked up working with PJ. She knew a delaying tactic when she saw one.

The girls met in the locker area, where Lisa changed into clean clothes. When she was finally ready, she looked up at her friends with a pale face.

"I don't feel so good," she said.

"You'll be fine," Carole told her. She knew Mr. Atwood was waiting, but she also knew no good would come of hurrying Lisa.

"Oh no," Lisa said, running into the bathroom. Stevie went with her and stayed with her while Lisa threw up.

"I can't see him; I'm sick," Lisa said.

"I think you're nervous," Stevie said. "Don't you feel better now?"

Lisa shook her head. Stevie knew she did feel better, though, because she was no longer sheet-colored.

"Come on, let's get you freshened up." She handed her some paper towels and brought her comb into the bathroom. Two minutes later, Lisa was ready to go.

"I'm coming over to your house for the sleepover tonight, right, Stevie?" she asked.

"Right," Stevie said. "And Carole and I promise not to say one word about horses until you get there. You won't miss a thing!"

Lisa smiled weakly. Stevie promised to look after her bags and told her to have a good time with her father. Lisa looked pained again.

"Lisa? Are you in there, honey?" It was a very familiar voice.

"Coming, Dad," she answered.

Lisa pulled open the door. There was her father, the same man she'd known all her life, the same Dad she'd loved all her life. He was still big, strong, and handsome, and he held his arms out to her for a hug.

The tears began even before she reached him.

LISA GOT TO Stevie's house about eight-thirty. Dinner was over, the dishes were done, and the usual riotous noise was echoing throughout the house. The major difference was that there was no backgammon game in progress. Mr. Lake was watching a documentary on television, and Mrs. Lake was on the phone, but she waved Lisa upstairs. Lisa made it to Stevie's room, barely missing a flying water balloon. Fortunately Alex caught it in spite of Chad's hard throw. Chad seemed very disappointed.

"Whoever misses has to clean it up," Chad explained.

Seemed perfectly logical to Lisa. She knocked on Stevie's door.

"Stay away, whoever you are!" Stevie grumbled.

"Unless you're Lisa," added Carole.

"Oh, I thought you were Michael," Stevie said, welcoming her friend.

"I figured as much," said Lisa, closing the door just before a balloon hit it and smashed.

"That's not fair!" Chad yowled. "It was a lousy throw!"

131

"No, it wasn't. It was a lousy catch!" Alex countered.

Lisa grimaced.

Stevie leaped for the door. "I'm going to give those brats a piece of my mind!" she snarled.

"Don't worry," Lisa said. "It's fine and they're just having fun—at least until your mother finds out."

"I suspect she already knows," said Stevie. "And maybe we're best off if we just leave the door closed." She backed off and returned to the pile of pillows she'd made on the floor.

Lisa flopped onto the bed.

"So?" Carole said. "Did you have a nice time?"

"That's the kind of question mothers ask," Lisa said, teasing.

"It must be my maternal instincts," Carol said. "Tell us how it went."

"It was fine," she said. "No, it was more than that. It was good."

"What did you do?" Stevie asked.

"Talked, mostly. I mean, we went out for pizza and then to the hotel where he's living now. But we talked. A lot. He wants me to know he loves me."

"Of course he loves you," Stevie said.

"It didn't feel like it much over the last week or two," Lisa said.

Stevie wished she hadn't said what she did, but Lisa

132

went on. "Look, it hurts," she told her friends. "It hurts more now than it did when it first happened."

"Maybe you just feel it more now," Carole suggested.

Lisa shrugged. "I told him about PJ. He said I'd done something important. He said one day, maybe, I could have my own horse. I don't think I want to own a horse, though. What if something happened to him?"

The question hung heavily in the room. Nobody had an answer for it.

"I wonder how the Wainwrights are doing in Oregon?" Carole asked.

"Who cares?" Stevie countered. The three of them shared a high five on that.

The talk turned easily to their favorite subject: Horses. They began by talking about their longeing lesson and then Veronica diAngelo's latest outrageous behavior, although they actually approved of it, since it seemed that Veronica had mistaken Mrs. Wainwright for a new stable hand. Pretty soon they were laughing about the silly mistakes the youngest riders were making and the mistakes they'd made themselves when they were beginners.

"I couldn't believe how many things Max expected me to remember to do at once!" Lisa laughed. "One time he told me eight things I was doing wrong all at the same time! You must have thought I was totally hopeless."

"No more than anyone else," said Carole. "Besides, even though we'd been riding for a while, I think he was telling us each five things at the same time."

"He doesn't miss anything, does he?" Lisa asked.

"Never!" said Carole. "Isn't he amazing?"

"He's the greatest!" Stevie agreed.

There was a knock on Stevie's door. "It's Mom," Mrs. Lake identified herself, probably to avoid being threatened with pillows the way Stevie usually greeted her brothers.

"Come on in," Stevie said.

Mrs. Lake entered, handing each of the girls a Popsicle. "We forgot dessert after dinner," she explained.

"Thanks," said Carole and Lisa, accepting the treats.

Mrs. Lake gave Stevie hers and then made a thumbs-up sign.

"Thanks, Mom," said Stevie.

"Good thinking and good night," said Mrs. Lake. She left the girls alone.

"What's that about?" Carole asked.

"Oh, nothing," said Stevie, but Lisa and Carole knew it wasn't true. Stevie was definitely up to something.

"I wonder how PJ is doing," Stevie said.

Carole winced a little, hoping the thought wouldn't upset Lisa. "I bet he's fine," she said. "He and Mr. Crawford seemed like a really good pair."

"Yeah, one who would let his horse run away," Lisa said.

"Through a fence that was hit by a car in the middle of the night," Stevie reminded her. "He really couldn't help that."

"Then why did he run so far?" Lisa asked.

"He's naturally skittish, you know. He might even have been hurt by the accident," said Stevie.

"Maybe," Lisa conceded.

"You know, Max said that there's a new mare coming to foal at Pine Hollow. I hope she's nice," Carole said, changing the subject. The stable kept a valuable stallion named Geronimo, and owners who wanted their mares to breed with him often had them deliver their foals at the stable so that they could be bred right after the foal was born.

"I love watching foals be born," Carole continued. "It's the most exciting thing in the world to think of the whole life that is in that funny-looking sac."

"Me too," said Lisa.

Carole was relieved to have successfully shifted the topic of conversation. No one mentioned PJ again that night.

STEVIE HAD A secret. She wasn't very good at keeping secrets, and she was glad she wasn't going to have to keep this one for very long. She was the first one up the next morning. Pretty soon the secret would be out.

"Come on, guys!" she said. "Day's a-wasting!"

"What do you mean, 'day's a-wasting'?" Carole asked, tossing her pillow at Stevie. "I just closed my eyes. It must be the middle of the night!"

"We don't have to be at Pine Hollow until ten this morning," Lisa reminded her, lofting her pillow across the room toward Stevie as well.

Stevie caught both pillows and dropped them to the floor.

"Time to get up. Just because we're not going to Pine Hollow doesn't mean we're not going someplace else," Stevie told her friends.

"What are you talking about?" Lisa asked, rubbing her eyes.

"This isn't one of those schemes where we have to help you with a science project, is it?" Carole asked.

"Nope," Stevie said. "It's something else altogether, and I'm not sure exactly when I'm going to tell you, but it certainly won't be when you're throwing things at me and accusing me of horrible acts." She was enjoying the suspense immensely.

"Okay, I'm curious," Carole said, turning to Lisa. "How about you?"

"Curious enough to get up," she admitted. Slowly, but faster than they really wanted, the girls got out of bed and began their morning.

Fifteen minutes later the three of them appeared in the Lakes' kitchen, where Mrs. Lake was flipping pancakes.

"Come on, Stevie, tell us now," Carole said.

"Oh, you haven't told them yet?" Mrs. Lake said. "I didn't think you'd be able to keep this secret for more than ten minutes."

"You're in on it?" Lisa asked.

"Not only am I in on it, but I'm driving!"

Mrs. Lake was no more forthcoming with the secret than her daughter had been. It wasn't until each girl had consumed two helpings of pancakes (plus bacon and orange juice), cleaned Stevie's room, gotten together all their riding gear, and hopped into the car that the secret was finally revealed.

"Well, we're going to Cross County," said Mrs. Lake, backing out of the driveway and checking some directions she'd scribbled on a piece of paper.

That was odd. Since Stevie's boyfriend, Phil Marsten, lived in Cross County, Mrs. Lake drove there frequently, and she certainly didn't need directions for that.

Then Carole remembered and knew that Lisa had never heard it so she wouldn't know.

"Really?" Carole asked. Stevie nodded excitedly, knowing her friend had figured it out. "How did you—"

"Mom called and asked," said Stevie. "He thought it was a great idea."

"You guys going to let me in on this little secret?" Lisa asked.

"I don't know," said Stevie, prolonging the fun. "It's not a long drive, but I brought a snack for you anyway." She handed her a brown paper lunch bag.

"After all those pancakes, I couldn't eat another thing!" Lisa protested.

"Well, it's not really for you," said Stevie. "Why don't you go ahead and see what it is."

Lisa peered into the crumpled bag. There was a sandwich inside, and she pulled it out. It was peanut butter and jelly. Then she understood.

"Really?" she asked.

"Really," said Stevie.

Lisa tried to keep the tears from her eyes, but it didn't work. Fortunately there was a napkin in the lunch bag as well.

It wasn't a long drive to Mr. Crawford's farm, and on their way Mrs. Lake told the girls how pleased Mr. Crawford was that they wanted to visit their late charge. He'd told her that Protocol was doing just fine and he'd surely be happy to see his friends.

Lisa listened, mostly pleased at the surprise Stevie and Mrs. Lake had planned for her. But she was also sad and a little bit worried at the same time. She knew she was still sad that PJ wasn't ever going to be hers. She was worried because she'd convinced herself that PJ's owner had mistreated him or he never would have run away, and she was afraid she might cry in front of Mr. Crawford. She blew her nose again and tried to collect herself. She was a mass of confused feelings, but she didn't have to let the whole world know it.

139

Mrs. Lake consulted the directions several more times before she finally turned into a long, tree-lined driveway. It was a real horse farm with wide-plank white board fences surrounding paddocks on either side of the drive. The fences had bordered the roadway for a good half mile before the house. Lisa remembered the story about the drunk driver hitting the fence. Maybe it wasn't such a crazy notion that Mr. Crawford might not have known for a couple of hours. They were big paddocks, and the road was far from the house.

PJ wasn't in either of those paddocks. Mrs. Lake continued up the drive to the house and stable. There were several cars parked in front of the house, plus the van that had been at Pine Hollow just over a week before. Mr. Crawford came out of the house and waved toward the Lakes' car even before it reached the house.

Lisa noticed for the first time that he had a nice smile.

"Welcome, caretakers!" he said as the girls climbed out of the car. "Now, you're Lisa, right?"

Lisa nodded. She couldn't help smiling back at him.

"And you're Stevie and Carole."

They shook his hand.

"And you must be Catherine Lake," he said, offering his hand to Stevie's mother. She shook it. "But of course, I'm not the reason you all came here, am I? Follow me." He led them to an exercise ring behind the barn.

140

Carole and Stevie let Lisa go first, and Mrs. Lake brought up the rear. Mr. Crawford chatted with Lisa as they walked together.

"He's doing just fine now. He was loose for a long time, almost six weeks, and those must have been tough times for him."

"We thought he got into a fight with a bobcat," Lisa said.

"Seems likely to me. Those are nasty scratches he has. He's going to have scars for the rest of his life."

"We did what we could to keep it from scarring," Lisa told him.

"Oh, I know you did everything. And from what I hear, you personally did most of it."

"I don't know about that," said Lisa. "Though I did try to help him. I got really worried when the scratches got so swollen and hot. Judy checked on him a lot, you know."

"I know," said Mr. Crawford. "He's right around this side of the barn," he said, pointing.

Lisa hesitated. PJ, her beloved PJ, was just around the corner. The problem was that the horse she was about to see wasn't actually named PJ, and he wasn't hers. She'd already forgotten about worrying that Mr. Crawford had abused him. It was clear that he really cared about his horse. Now the only thing Lisa worried about was how much it was going to hurt her to see him again.

She rounded the corner. It was a nice little exercise ring, about the size of Pine Hollow's jumping ring. PJ was there. He'd found a shady spot and was nibbling at some sweet sprouts of grass.

"PJ!" she called. He kept on nibbling. "I've got something for you!" His ears flicked. His jaw chomped. He stayed where he was.

Lisa climbed up one rung of the fence. "Here, boy!" she called. She reached into the brown paper bag and took out the peanut butter and jelly sandwich. The horse lifted his head and sniffed the air.

Mr. Crawford stood nearby. He whistled. The horse snorted, then trotted over to the fence.

"I guess Protocol's just used to me," the man said.

"Thanks," Lisa told him. "Do I have to call him Protocol?"

"You can call him whatever you're comfortable with," said Mr. Crawford. "And if you are planning on sharing that sandwich with him, I think he'll be calling you sweetheart. You know, he's just bonkers about peanut butter. My wife gave him some one time and he's never lost his taste for it."

"You're kidding," said Lisa.

"He loves the stuff. Go ahead, you'll see."

"I already did," Lisa said. "That's why I call him PJ."

142

Mr. Crawford laughed. "Nobody told me you'd discovered his secret passion. No wonder he behaved for you! He can be pretty naughty, you know."

"Unless you're grooming him or feeding him," said Lisa, smiling at their shared knowledge.

"It's like you read his mind," said Mr. Crawford.

By then PJ had arrived, demanding his treat and tolerating the affection that Lisa showered on him. He was obliging as long as the sandwich lasted.

Half an hour later, The Saddle Club and Mrs. Lake were back in the car, heading to Pine Hollow in time for their jump class. At first nobody spoke, because everyone was waiting for Lisa to say something, and she was still busy sorting out her emotions.

"Thank you, Mrs. Lake and Stevie," she said.

"You're welcome, Lisa," Mrs. Lake responded. "It was Stevie's idea."

"Of course," said Lisa. Stevie was always the one to come up with the finest (though sometimes weirdest) plans.

"I thought you were upset," Stevie said. "But it worked out okay, didn't it?"

"I was and it did," Lisa said. "You know, it was a little bit the way it was with my dad yesterday. I was nervous about seeing him, but it was fine."

143

"Fine?" Carole asked.

"More than fine," Lisa said. "Great."

"Mr. Crawford said you could come ride PJ sometime when his leg is all better," said Stevie. "Would you like to do that?"

"I don't know," Lisa said. "When I saw him again today, I realized that he's not an easy horse to get along with. When I was taking care of him, I felt so sorry for him that I never stopped to realize how much he misbehaved. I'd rather think of him happily chomping on a peanut butter and jelly sandwich than bucking me out of the saddle!"

"Pine Hollow Station," Mrs. Lake announced, pulling into the stable driveway.

The girls thanked her for the sleepover, the visit to Mr. Crawford's, and the ride. Then they dashed off to saddle up their horses.

14

"I CAN'T GO for a trail ride this afternoon," Lisa said to her friends two weeks later when they were all at the stable again.

"Aw, come on!" said Stevie.

"Dad's picking me up," she said. "I haven't seen him for two weeks, and I have so much to tell him."

Stevie was immediately embarrassed at her gaffe. Of course an afternoon with Lisa's father was more important than a trail ride.

"Sure, I understand," she said. "You can tell him about seeing PJ."

"That, and about a million other things. We talked last night. He's still staying at that hotel, but he says he'll have an apartment soon, and when he does, I can stay over with him. Maybe you guys could come, too."

Stevie thought that might feel weird. "Really?"

"Of course," she said. "He already told me."

"Okay," Stevie said.

"And you're going to be away with him every other Saturday?" Carole asked.

"That's what they worked out for now—until he gets an apartment. Then it'll change a little."

"But you're going to miss all kinds of riding," Stevie said.

"It's only every other weekend," Lisa reminded her. "And he's going to get an apartment nearby so that I can come to Pine Hollow on Saturdays, too."

"What about him moving to California?" Carole asked.

"I don't know," said Lisa. "He may, he may not. But if he does, we'll figure something out. I'm not going to be able to fly across the country every other weekend! Come on, I've got to change."

The girls followed her into the locker area. It felt like a lot longer than two weeks ago that the three of them had been there waiting for Lisa to talk to her dad the last time. Lisa was more relaxed and even eager to see her father. She wasn't nervous, angry, or sick to her stomach.

"Too bad we can't visit PJ this weekend," Stevie said.

"Oh, he's doing fine, I'm sure," said Lisa, picking up a towel. "I called Mr. Crawford on Wednesday. He said the leg has healed and he's even ridden him a couple of times. That horse doesn't need us anymore." She picked up a bar of soap and headed to the bathroom to wash up.

"That was interesting," said Stevie.

"Definitely," Carole agreed. "I guess that story Mrs. Reg told us about the pony was right. PJ is totally readjusted and doing fine. He's where he belongs."

"*That's* not what Mrs. Reg's story was about," Stevie said, looking curiously at her friend.

"Sure sounded like it to me," said Carole.

"No," Stevie said. "I don't think so. I think she was telling us that Lisa was going to get better once she got used to her new family arrangement. The changes she's been going through have been just as upsetting as the horse's, and now she's doing pretty well."

"Yeah, she is," said Carole. "She was pretty weird there for a while."

Lisa emerged from the bathroom then, stopping that particular conversation. They chatted while she dressed, and when her dad called into the locker area to say he was there to pick her up, she was ready.

"Be right there, Dad," she said. She slid her backpack onto her shoulder.

"Have fun with your father," Carole said.

"Of course I will," Lisa said. Then she added, "He's my dad!"

When she left the room, Stevie and Carole looked at each other and smiled.

"Another successful Saddle Club project," Stevie declared.

They shared a high five.

148

ABOUT THE AUTHOR

BONNIE BRYANT is the author of more than a hundred books about horses, including The Saddle Club series, The Saddle Club Super Editions, the Pony Tails series, and Pine Hollow, which follows the Saddle Club girls into their teens. She has also written novels and movie novelizations under her married name, B. B. Hiller.

Ms. Bryant began writing The Saddle Club in 1986. Although she had done some riding before that, she intensified her studies then and found herself learning right along with her characters Stevie, Carole, and Lisa. She claims that they are all much better riders than she is.

Ms. Bryant was born and raised in New York City. She still lives there, in Greenwich Village, with her two sons.

Don't miss the next exciting
Saddle Club adventure . . .

Best Friends
Saddle Club #101

Christmas is coming, and The Saddle Club is busily getting ready for an exciting holiday show. But part of their preparation involves raising money—a lot of it! When Lisa realizes that Carole and Stevie are having a hard time coming up with the cash, she takes matters into her own hands. At the same time, Carole and Stevie are secretly plotting to help each other. Will The Saddle Club be able to fix this funding fiasco in time for the show?

Meanwhile, a winter storm is brewing that may give the girls even more trouble. When things get rough, The Saddle Club must work together harder than ever to prove that the strength of friendship can get them through even the toughest times.

MEET
the SADDLE CLUB

Horse lover CAROLE . . .
Practical joker STEVIE . . .
Straight-A LISA . . .

THE SADDLE CLUB
SUPER EDITIONS

THE SADDLE CLUB
SPECIAL EDITIONS